'The scen [...]
very simp [...]

Max continued, [...] g widow—bravely struggling to support her small daughter—agrees to marry the wealthy prince and they both live happily ever after. A deeply romantic story. And one guaranteed to bring a tear to the eye of the most hardened cynic.'

It was some moments before Amber was fully able to comprehend what he was saying.

'You must be crazy!' she gasped.

'On the contrary it makes perfect sense. My daughter clearly needs a father. And I'm *quite* determined that she's going to have one.'

Dear Reader

It's Christmas-time again, the season of love and sharing—and on that theme we have included in this, our Christmas collection, four new heart-warming seasonal novels, by internationally acclaimed authors, where romance is very much in the air. And whether this collection is a present to yourself or a gift to you from a loved one, then we hope that these romances will bring joy into your heart at this special time of year.

Wishing you a very happy Christmas.

The Editors

Mary Lyons was born in Toronto, Canada, moving to live permanently in England when she was six, although she still proudly maintains her Canadian citizenship. Having married and raised four children, her life nowadays is relatively peaceful—unlike her earlier years when she worked as a radio announcer, reviewed books and, for a time, lived in a turbulent area of the Middle East. She still enjoys a bit of excitement, combining romance with action, humour and suspense in her books whenever possible.

Recent titles by the same author:

IT STARTED WITH A KISS

YULETIDE BRIDE

BY
MARY LYONS

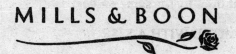

MILLS & BOON

All the characters in this book have no existence outside the imagination of the author, and have no relation whatsoever to anyone bearing the same name or names. They are not even distantly inspired by any individual known or unknown to the author, and all the incidents are pure invention.

*MILLS & BOON and the Rose Device
are trademarks of the publisher.
Harlequin Mills & Boon Limited,
Eton House, 18-24 Paradise Road, Richmond, Surrey, TW9 1SR
This edition published by arrangement with Harlequin Enterprises B.V.*

© Mary Lyons 1995

ISBN 0 263 79280 3

*Set in Times Roman 10.5 on 12pt
94-9511-53908 C*

Made and printed in Great Britain

CHAPTER ONE

'I'M SORRY to be late,' Amber called out breathlessly as she made her way through the noisy, crowded café, to where her friend was sitting at a small table beside the window.

'There was no need to hurry,' Rose Thomas told her, before ordering a pot of coffee from a passing waitress. 'Sally hasn't arrived yet. If I know her, she's probably spending a fortune in one of the dress shops. *And* busy catching up on all the latest scandal, of course!'

'I expect you're right,' Amber grinned. Their friend Sally, the wife of a wealthy and highly respected lawyer, was affectionately known amongst her friends as being both a shop-aholic, and an avid collector of local news and gossip. 'But, as far as I'm concerned,' she added, sighing with relief as she lowered her carrier bags and parcels down on to the floor, 'trying to do any ordinary, everyday shopping during the run-up to Christmas, is nothing but sheer murder.'

'Don't I know it!' Rose agreed with a rueful laugh. 'Even though it's only Thursday, the supermarket was packed as tight as a tin of sardines, and I didn't manage to buy half the things on my shopping list. Since my dreaded mother-in-law is threatening to descend on us for the Christmas holidays, I was just wondering if I could ask you to make me a large plum pudding? And maybe some sponge cakes to keep in the freezer just in case of any unexpected visitors?'

'No problem—all orders gratefully received!' Amber grinned as she pulled out a chair and sat down.

'That'll be wonderful,' Rose sighed with relief. 'By the way, how is your business doing?'

'Well, it looks as though I'm going to be very busy in the kitchen, since I've now got lots of orders from the local shops for Christmas cakes, puddings and mince pies. Unfortunately, the paying-guest side of the business isn't doing so well. Bookings are down, and we don't have anyone staying with us at the moment. On top of which...' she hesitated for a moment. 'I don't want anyone else to know just yet, because I'm still trying to summon up enough courage to break the bad news to my mother. However, after a really awful interview with the bank manager, I've finally had to face the hard, financial facts of life and put my house on the market.'

'You don't mean...?'

Amber nodded. 'Yes, I'm afraid so. I've seen Mr Glover, the house agent, and the Hall is going to be advertised for sale as from the beginning of next week.'

'Oh, no! I'm *so* sorry,' Rose exclaimed, gazing at her friend with deep concern and sympathy. Since they'd both been born and raised in the same small, riverside market town of Elmbridge, she was well aware of the misfortunes suffered in the past by Amber's family; the public scandal and disgrace surrounding the crash of her father's large business empire, swiftly followed by his death and her mother's complete mental breakdown. It seemed so desperately unfair, Rose told herself, that after all the trials and tribulations which she'd so bravely confronted in the past, her friend should now be having to face yet even more problems.

'Oh, well—it's not exactly the end of the world. The Hall is far too large for us, and the heating bills are astronomical,' Amber pointed out, attempting to put a brave face on what was, in reality, a disastrous family situation.

'But where will you go?' Rose asked anxiously as the waitress brought a tray to their table. 'Have you found anywhere else to live?'

Amber sighed. 'No, not yet. I'm hoping to buy a small cottage, not too far away from Elmbridge. Mainly, of course, because I don't want to take Lucy away from either her school, or her friends.'

'I'll keep my ear to the ground, and let you know the moment I hear of anything,' Rose assured her earnestly. However, as she poured them both a cup of coffee, she couldn't help worrying about how her friend would manage to cope with life in a small cottage.

She'd been away at college when Amber, at the age of eighteen, had married Clive Stanhope, a very wealthy if somewhat wild young man, who'd owned Elmbridge Hall, an ancient Tudor mansion and by far the largest house in the district. Clive's wedding to Amber—the once rich, but by then penniless only child of a disgraced businessman—followed by the birth of a daughter only six months after their marriage, had provided plenty of ammunition for gossip in the small town. However, Amber had subsequently won everyone's admiration by the way she'd coped after her husband's fatal car accident, a year later, when it became known that Clive had apparently been a compulsive gambler, and all the land was heavily mortgaged. In fact, after everything had been sold to meet a mountain of debts, the young widow had been left with nothing but Elmbridge Hall.

Over the past few years, Rose had looked forward to a time when her friend would meet the right man and live happily ever after. With thick shoulder-length straight hair, a glorious shade of deep golden brown, and large green eyes set above a warm generous mouth, Amber was a very beautiful woman. Certainly Philip Jackson, the young local doctor, seemed to think so. But, despite all her matchmaking efforts, Rose couldn't understand why her friend—who was also a loving mother and superb cook—appeared to be so reluctant to get married again. But now . . . well, surely Amber would see the sense in marrying a man who had so much to offer her?

'I saw Philip Jackson the other day. He tells me that he's going to his parents' home in Cumberland for Christmas.'

'Oh, yes?' Amber murmured, eyeing her friend warily.

'Well, I was just wondering if . . . er . . . if he's asked you and Lucy to join him?'

'For Heaven's sake—don't you *ever* give up?' Amber groaned, shaking her head in mock exasperation. 'I thought you'd promised to stop trying to marry me off to all the single men in town?'

'Yes, well...' Rose's cheeks reddened slightly. 'I really don't mean to interfere in your life. But it's almost seven years since Clive died. And it's as clear as daylight to me—especially after hearing the sad news about the sale of your house—that what you *really* need is a husband.'

'I hope you're not suggesting that I should marry Philip—or anyone else, for that matter—merely to provide a way out of my difficulties?' Amber demanded bluntly.

'No—of course, I'm not,' Rose protested, waving a hand dismissively in the air. 'But surely this is the perfect time to think seriously about your future?'

'Oh, come on, Rose! We're not just talking about me. There's Lucy to consider, as well. It's not everyone who'd want to take on a little seven-year-old girl— not to mention my scatty mother.'

'I know your mother can be a problem at times,' Rose agreed, well aware that Violet Grant, who'd never really recovered from the trauma of her husband's sudden death, was an extra and often tiresome burden for the young widow's slim shoulders to carry. 'But Philip is clearly mad about you, and you can't deny that he'd be a really good choice of stepfather for Lucy. On top of which, I happen to think that you'd make a *marvellous* doctor's wife.'

Amber smiled and shook her head. 'Thanks for the vote of confidence! I know you mean well, and that what you're saying probably makes sense, but... OK, OK, I promise to give the matter some thought,' she added hurriedly as her old friend seemed determined to press the point. 'Now, tell me—is your mother-in-law going to be staying for the *whole* of the Christmas holidays?' she asked, firmly changing the subject. Unfortunately, there was no way she could tell Rose the truth; that having already made one marriage of convenience—although Clive Stanhope had been a very kind, generous-hearted man—she was desperately wary of entering into such an arrangement ever again.

To be fair, her friend did have a point about Lucy. Ever since Clive had died, when her daughter was just under a year old, she had done her best to be both mother and father to the little girl. That she hadn't always succeeded in properly fulfilling the two, very different roles over the past seven years, was a fact of which Amber was becoming daily more aware. So, maybe Rose was right? Maybe she ought to stop shilly-shallying, and force herself to take the practical, sensible decision to marry Philip Jackson?

A highly respected doctor, who'd recently joined a local practice, Philip was a genuinely nice and considerate man. The fact that he also had a private income, lived in a large house all on his own and was reasonably good-looking, with fair hair and kind brown eyes, made him the obvious candidate as far as her friends were concerned. But, while she was very fond of Philip, she wasn't in love with him. And having once experienced the intense, tempestuous drive of overwhelming emotion and desire, it seemed quite wrong to settle for second best.

' . . . so, the old dragon is bound to make Christmas a misery for all of us, and . . . *Good Heavens*! It looks as if Sally really *has* been spending a fortune!'

Startled by Rose's sudden exclamation, and guiltily aware that while she'd been buried deep in thought, she'd missed most of what her friend had been saying, Amber looked up to see a petite blonde woman making her way towards them, her progress impeded by the enormous amount of parcels she was carrying.

'Hi, darlings! I'm sorry to be so late,' she cried. 'I've never known the shops to be so crowded. But I know you'll both forgive me when I tell you some absolutely *riveting* news!'

'I don't know why you aren't running your own gossip column in the local newspaper!' Rose mocked as she and Amber exchanged a quick grin with one another.

'Oh, don't be so stuffy,' Sally laughed good-naturedly, placing her shopping on an adjacent chair as she sat down to join them. 'Besides, this isn't a rumour—it's the genuine truth, which everyone will know about sooner or later,' she added before turning to Amber. 'Do you remember Lady Parker? The mega-rich old woman that lived near you, and who died in a big fire at her house well over a year ago?'

Amber nodded. 'I never actually met the old lady, because she'd been a recluse for many years. Apparently the house was burned to the ground.'

'Right. Well, my dear husband was in charge of her affairs, and it seems that she always refused to make a will,' Sally continued excitedly. 'So, it took John simply *ages* to track down her only living relative. However, he's now finally succeeded, and Lady Parker's ten thousand acres—plus goodness knows how much extra money in stocks and shares, has all been inherited by...''Mad Max''!'

'*What*?' Rose gasped in astonishment. 'You don't mean...? Not...not the old vicar's son—Max Warner?'

'Yes!' Sally beamed at her friends, delighted at the expression of shock and surprise on their faces. Amber, in particular, appeared to be totally stunned.

'I just *knew* that you'd both be amazed to hear about the return of our old school heart-throb,' she continued happily. 'Of course, it's been years since the Reverend Augustus Warner died, so I suppose that it's not surprising that we'd forgotten all about his son. When John first told me about the return of ''Mad Max'', I could hardly believe my ears!'

'He certainly deserved that nickname!' Rose laughed. 'I remember him as a wild tearaway—with a simply *terrible* reputation for breaking girls' hearts. All the same...' she paused, staring into space with a dreamy expression on her face. 'Max really *was* diabolically attractive, wasn't he?'

'Absolutely scrumptious!' Sally agreed with a grin. 'In fact, with his curly black hair and those twinkling, wicked blue eyes, the effect on our young teenage hearts was completely *lethal*!'

'Mmm...' Rose gave a sheepish grin. 'After he kissed me at my sixteenth birthday party, I can remember being madly in love with Max for a whole year.'

'Weren't we all?' her friend sighed heavily. 'Of course, Amber is two years younger than either of us, and so probably won't recall any of the completely crazy things he used to get up to. Do you remember that huge black motorbike of his? And the really *ferocious* competition amongst us girls, as to who could wangle a ride behind him on the pillion seat?'

'Oh, yes! One of the highlights of my teens was when he once took me down the motorway at well over a hundred miles an hour.' Cheeks flushed, Rose shook her head at her own folly. 'I was absolutely scared to death, of course. But it was worth it. I reckoned I was the envy of everyone at school for at least two whole weeks!'

Sally giggled. 'You certainly were. I can remember Cynthia Henderson, for instance, collapsing into a jealous fit of raving hysterics—right in the middle of school assembly!'

'It's all very well to talk about old school days, but where's Max been all these years?' Rose asked. 'I know he was very clever. And, despite fooling around, he passed his school exams with flying colours before gaining a scholarship to university. But his father, old Reverend Warner, died while I was away training to be a nurse—and I've never heard anything about Max from that day to this.'

'Nor had anyone else,' Sally agreed. 'In fact, my dear husband had almost given up the search for him. And then...when he was invited to a very grand, fund-raising dinner in London a few weeks ago, he discovered that Max Warner was the principal guest speaker!'

'Good Heavens!'

'We all thought that Max had dropped off the edge of the world, didn't we? But not a bit of it!' Sally gave a loud peal of laughter. 'It seems he had an uncle in America. So, when his father died eight years ago, Max went off to the States to make his fortune. He's now returned to England as the terrifically successful, managing director of a huge, high-powered public company. *And* he's made an appointment to see John sometime soon, here in Elmbridge. *How about that*!'

While her friends were chatting excitedly together, exchanging news of a long-lost old school friend, Amber had been sitting rigidly still, her mind dazed and reeling, as though she'd been hit on the back of her head by a heavy sandbag. Even Sally's sudden shriek of horror hardly managed to penetrate her stunned brain.

'Oh, help—just look at the time!' Sally quickly jumped up from the table. 'I should have been at the hairdresser's at least ten minutes ago!'

'What an extraordinary piece of news about Max Warner,' Rose mused as Sally bustled out of the café, before catching sight of her friend's chalk-white face and dazed, stricken expression.

'*Amber*! What on earth's wrong? Are you all right?'

'Yes, I...' She took a deep breath and tried to pull herself together. 'Really, I'm fine,' she shakily informed Rose, who was gazing at her with deep concern.

'You've been trying to do too much,' her friend pointed out firmly. 'Having to cope with your mother is enough to try the patience of a saint! And running that huge old house...'

'I'm sorry...I have to go. I really must get home...there's so much cooking to do....' Amber muttered breathlessly as she swiftly gathered up her parcels.

'You don't look at all well. I hope you're not going down with flu?' Her friend gazed with concern at Amber's pale face and trembling figure. 'If you're not feeling too good, there's no need to worry about picking up Emily from school tomorrow. I can easily put off my trip to London.'

'No... don't do that. I'm fine. I've just got a lot to do today—that's all,' she assured Rose, before hurriedly making her way out of the café.

Dazed and shivering with nervous tension, Amber sat huddled in the front seat of her ancient Land Rover, staring blindly at the wind-rippled, dark water of the wide river estuary. Completely shattered by Sally's news, she'd known that there was no way she was in a fit state to drive the five miles back to Elmbridge Hall. Not when it had taken her several fumbled attempts to even place her key in the ignition. But since she couldn't continue sitting in the town car park, either, she'd cautiously made her way down to the quayside which was, as she'd hoped, completely deserted at this time of year.

She ought to have *known* that this was likely to happen sooner or later, Amber told herself grimly, wrapping her arms tightly about her trembling figure. What a blind, stupid fool she had been—living in a fool's paradise for the past eight years. While she'd had no idea that Lady Parker was his grandmother, she *should* have realised that Max Warner must eventually return—like the prodigal son—to his old home town of Elmbridge.

Suddenly feeling in need of some fresh air, Amber opened the door and stepped down from the Land Rover. Walking slowly up and down over the frosty cobblestones, she desperately tried to clear her mind, to try and work out what she was going to do. But it was proving difficult to think clearly when her mind seemed to be filled with memories of the past.

A much-loved and only child of wealthy parents, Amber had always been protected from the harsh facts of life. But the catastrophic events surrounding the collapse of her father's business empire, during the long hot summer of her eighteenth birthday, had shattered and destroyed for ever the safe, secure world of her childhood. Shocked and bewildered by the newspaper headlines trumpeting 'Financial Scandal!' and 'Millions Lost by Suffolk Businessman!' she'd been totally ill-equipped to deal with either the devastating news of her father's bankruptcy, or his sudden death from a fatal heart attack. And when her mother—unable to face the prospect of either being shunned by her former friends, or the total reverse of the family fortunes—had collapsed and been placed by the family doctor in a local psychiatric nursing home, Amber had found herself standing completely alone amidst the ashes of her previous existence.

Maybe if, during that tense and anxious time, there had been someone with whom she could have discussed her problems, her life might have turned out differently. But with no close relations other than an elderly aunt in London, and all her school friends either away on holiday—or prevented by their cautious parents from associating with the child of a man who had, reportedly, been involved in crooked financial dealings—her only relief from the mounting stress and strain had been to take long, solitary walks through the deserted meadows edging the river-bank near her home. And there it was that Max had found her, one hot afternoon in late August, weeping with despair and deep unhappiness.

Despite an early teenage crush on the wickedly glamorous Max Warner, she'd seen nothing of him during the past five years. However, it had seemed the most natural thing in the world when he'd put his strong arms about her trembling figure.

'How could I have forgotten those wonderful, sparkling green eyes?' he'd said, smiling lazily down at her as he wiped away her tears. 'I always knew that you'd grow up to become a real beauty.'

'Have I really...?' she'd gasped, her cheeks flushing hectically beneath his warm, engaging smile as he gently brushed the long, damp tendrils of hair from her wide brow, before lowering his dark head to softly kiss her trembling lips.

Miraculously, it seemed that Max—unlike so many of her family's friends and acquaintances—did not hold her personally responsible for her father's misdeeds. And as they'd walked slowly back to her house, whose contents were now mostly in packing cases for despatch to the local saleroom, she realised that he, too, was suffering from the sudden loss of a parent. Completely immersed in her own problems, Amber had only been dimly aware of the Reverend Warner's recent death from a massive stroke, resulting in Max's urgent recall from America, where he'd just completed his postgraduate degree at the Harvard Business School. However, when he confessed to the misery and desolation of being now alone in large empty rooms of the vicarage, or his deep regret at not having been closer to his father, saying, 'I was pretty wild as a teenager, and there's no doubt he must have found me a considerable pain in the neck,' she was easily able to understand Max's thoughts and feelings at such an unhappy time.

If *only* she hadn't been quite so young and innocent! Amber squirmed with embarrassment as she now gazed back down the years at her youthful self. With her head stuffed full of romantic fantasies, her dazed mind reeling beneath the assault of those glittering blue eyes and his overwhelming sensual attraction, it was no wonder that—like some modern-day Cinderella—she'd immediately fallen head over heels in love with her very own Prince Charming. But if Max found her obvious adoration a nuisance, he gave no indication of doing so, as day after day he joined her for long walks along the deserted river-bank. So, it was perhaps inevitable that, having tripped and fallen over a log hidden in the thick grass, she should have found herself clasped in his arms, fervently responding to the fiercely determined possession of his lips and body.

It wasn't for lack of trying, of course. But, over the past eight years, Amber had never been able to fool herself into believing that Max was totally to blame for what happened. Pathetically ignorant of lovemaking as she was, the feverish impetus of her desire had been every bit as strong as his, her ardent and passionate response clearly overpowering any scruples he may have had.

It had always seemed to Amber as if the next few weeks had been an all too brief, halcyon period of enchantment and rapture. Neither the deep sadness of her father's death, nor her increasing worries about her mother's mental condition, had seemed to disturb their mutual ecstasy and euphoric happiness, or the uncontrollable desire that exploded between them each and every time they were able to be alone with one another.

Unfortunately, there was nothing they could do to prevent the harsh, cruel light of reality from eventually breaking through their cloud of happiness. Both the fast-approaching sale of her family home, and the offer to Max of a job in his uncle's large firm in America, meant that they would soon have to part.

Starry-eyed with joy when he placed a small gold ring on her finger, vowing that they would be married just as soon as he was well established in his new career, Amber had never doubted Max's total sincerity. 'My uncle's offering me a good salary, with a partnership in the near future. So, it won't be long before we can be together for ever and ever,' he'd pledged, clasping her tightly in his arms before leaving for the airport. 'Just promise that you'll wait for me?'

'Of course I will,' she told him fervently, blinking rapidly in order to prevent the weak tears from running down her cheeks as she waved him goodbye.

And she *had* waited. Waiting, alone in the empty house through the long autumn days, while her father's creditors checked that all her family's precious possessions had been sold; waiting, while her mother who, if not yet ready to leave the hospital, was showing definite signs of improvement. Until, well over two months after his departure, her increasing apprehension that she might be pregnant hardened into certainty, and she realised that she was in deep and desperate trouble....

A sudden, freezing gust of wind cut into her memories of that intensely unhappy time, bringing her sharply back to her present-day problems—and the questions raised by the fear of Max's return. However, by the time she found herself driving back home, Amber had managed to regain a small measure of self-control.

She couldn't, of course, pretend that Max's return was likely to be anything other than a major disaster. On the other hand, to have found herself in such a blind panic, feeling sick and shivering like a leaf at the mere sound of his name, wasn't going to achieve anything, either. Leaving her own desperate worry and fears about Lucy aside, it was plainly quite ridiculous of her to have been so overcome with sheer terror. Max may have inherited Lady Parker's large estate— but so what? If, as Sally had said, he was enjoying such a successful career in London, and only visiting Elmbridge to meet his grandmother's lawyer, there was very little likelihood of his ever returning to live permanently in the area. Besides... all this frantic shock and worry could well prove to be completely unfounded. It was more than likely that such an attractive, vital man would be married by now, and have completely forgotten all about their very brief, secret love affair.

As she made her way up the drive, she was comforted by the familiar sight of the ancient mansion with its warm red brick and mullioned windows, which, despite its imminent sale, seemed at the moment to offer a place of refuge and safety.

An American guest had once referred enthusiastically to Elmbridge Hall as a 'Medieval Gem'. He may have been right, Amber thought wryly as she carried her shopping into the house, but he should try living here in the winter! Which was yet another reason for selling this huge, rambling old house, she reminded herself grimly, only too well aware of the astonomically high bills for coal and electricity, which would be due for payment in the new year.

'Hello, dear. Are you going out shopping?' her mother murmured, wandering into the hall and casting an approving glance at her daughter's old tweed coat, over a matching skirt and green, polo-necked sweater, the same colour as her eyes.

Stifling a sigh, Amber explained that, far from going anywhere, she had just returned with the shopping—before once again reminding the older woman of the large note pad and pencil beside the telephone.

'Mother! Do *please* try and concentrate,' she added, as Violet Grant drifted about the hall, idly touching up a flower decoration here, and straightening an oil painting there. 'I've got a huge order for plum puddings. So, I'm going to shut myself away in the kitchen until it's time to collect Lucy from school. As I won't be able to hear the phone here in the hall, I'm relying on you to take down any bookings. It's *very* important that you write down the correct names and the exact dates they want to stay with us—OK?'

'There's no need to worry, dear.' Violet Grant gave her daughter an injured look. 'You know that I always do my best to welcome your friends to the house.'

Amber closed her eyes for a moment, mentally counting up to ten. While she loved her mother very dearly, there was no doubt that even her seven-year-old daughter, Lucy, seemed to have a stronger grasp on reality than poor Violet. Unfortunately, the older woman seemed incapable of understanding either the family's dire need for hard cash, or the necessity of accurately recording all telephone messages.

A child of wealthy parents, and much indulged by her rich husband, Violet's butterfly mind had never been able to fully accept their changed circumstances. Even though it was now a long time since all the scandal and newspaper headlines, which had surrounded both the crash of her husband's business empire and his subsequent fatal heart attack, Violet continued to live in a private world of her own.

Four years ago, when Amber had first floated the idea of taking in paying guests, her mother had been distraught.

'You must have taken leave of your senses!' Violet had gasped in horror, before collapsing down on to a chair. 'To think that I should live to see my own daughter running a...a *boarding-house*!'

'Oh, come on, Mother—it's hardly the end of the world!' Amber had retorted with exasperation. While she felt sorry for the older woman, she nevertheless knew that they both had to face up to the harsh facts of life. 'When poor Clive died, he left us with nothing but this house and a huge pile of debts. We've sold everything we can, and now that Lucy is growing up, she's going to be needing clothes and toys, and lots of other things that we simply can't afford at the moment. The house is our only asset, which is why I've decided to take in paying guests. However, if you can think of an alternative plan of action—I'll be glad to hear it!'

Not able to come up with a viable course of action, it seemed the only way Violet Grant could cope with their changed status was to completely close her mind to what she called the 'sordid, financial aspects' of Amber's business. However, by insisting on treating those who came to the house as personal guests of her daughter—charmingly welcoming everyone as if they were old family friends—Violet had, in many ways, proved to be a considerable asset.

But that state of affairs was now coming to an end, Amber quickly reminded herself as she made her way to the kitchen, feeling distinctly guilty at not yet having found the courage to tell her mother about the forthcoming sale of the Hall. She was deeply ashamed of being such a coward—but dreaded having to face the hysterical scenes that were bound to follow such bad news.

All the same . . . she told herself some time later as she moistened the heavy, dried-fruit pudding mixture

with a hefty dose of brandy, she *really* couldn't put
off telling her mother the truth for much longer. As
for the question of Max's return—well, the sooner
she put it out of her mind, the better. After all, no
one had any idea of what had happened during that
long, hot summer over eight years ago. So, there was
no reason why the episode shouldn't remain firmly
buried in the mists of time.

Continuing to sternly lecture herself throughout the
rest of the day and most of the next, Amber had
gradually managed to recover her usual good sense
and equilibrium. Being busily occupied in trying to
catch up with all her orders for home-made Christmas
produce was proving to be a positive advantage, since
she simply didn't have time to think about anything
other than the job in hand. Only abandoning the
kitchen to collect Lucy and her friend, Emily Thomas,
from school, she was delighted when they decided that
it would be fun to explore the contents of some of
her mother's old trunks up in the attic. There was
nothing that Lucy liked more than dressing up in
Violet's old clothes—a fact that Amber welcomed,
since it meant that the little girls were happily occupied while she made another batch of mince pies
for the freezer.

Busily absorbed by her work in the kitchen, she was
startled when one of the row of old-fashioned bells
began ringing high on the wall above her head.

Glancing up, she noted with surprise that there was
obviously someone at the front door. Certainly Rose,
on a shopping trip to Cambridge, wouldn't be col-

lecting Emily for another hour at least—and she couldn't think of anyone else likely to be calling at this time of day. However, as the bell was given yet another impatient ring, she realised that she was going to have to go and answer it.

Wondering who on earth it could be, Amber didn't bother to remove her messy apron as she hurried down the dark corridor, through the green baize door, which separated the kitchen quarters from the rest of the house, and across the stone floor of the large hall.

'OK, OK, I'm coming!' she muttered under her breath as someone began banging loudly on the old oak door.

'I'm sorry to keep you waiting...' she began as she opened the door. And then, almost reeling with shock, she found herself frantically clutching the large brass door handle for support. With the blood draining from her face, her dazed and confused mind seemed barely able to comprehend the evidence of her own eyes. Because there—standing casually on the doorstep beside Mr Glover, the house agent—was the tall dark figure of Max Warner!

CHAPTER TWO

JABBING a fork into the iron-hard frosty ground, Amber tried to ignore the bitterly cold wind gusting through the large kitchen garden. Saving money by growing their own fruits and vegetables was all very well, but having to dig up leeks and parsnips in the middle of winter wasn't exactly one of her favourite pastimes.

On the other hand, she'd always found that there was nothing like a bout of hard digging or hoeing to put any problems she might have in their correct perspective. Unfortunately, it didn't seem to be working at the moment, Amber told herself gloomily, pausing for a moment to brush a lock of golden brown hair from her troubled green eyes.

What on earth was she going to do? It was a question that she had been asking herself, with increasing desperation, ever since she'd discovered Max Warner—together with the house agent, Mr Glover—standing on her front doorstep. Even now, two weeks later, there seemed nothing she could do to calm her tense, edgy body, while her brain appeared to be frozen rigid with fright. In fact, with her nerves at screaming point, she wasn't able to think about *anything*, other than Max's sudden reappearance in her life—which had to be one of the most catastrophic and potentially disastrous twists of fate she'd ever experienced!

She'd hardly been able to believe the evidence of her own eyes. Almost paralytic with shock, the breath driven from her body as if from a hard blow to the solar plexus, it had taken her some moments to realise that it truly *was* Max, and not an evil figment of her overheated imagination.

'Good afternoon, Mrs Stanhope. It was very good of you to agree to see my client at such short notice,' the estate agent had murmured pompously, his voice seeming to be coming from somewhere far away. 'I...er...I hope you haven't forgotten our appointment?' he added hesitantly, gazing with apprehension at the young woman, who was staring silently at both him and Mr Warner in such a wide-eyed, unnerving manner.

'An appointment...?' Amber echoed helplessly, her mind in a chaotic whirl as she stared past him to where a sleek, glossy black sports car was parked beside Mr Glover's vehicle on the gravelled drive outside the house. 'I don't understand. Do...do you mean you want to see over the house?'

'Yes, of course.' Mr Glover gave a nervous laugh, clearly wondering if the young widow was entirely 'all there'. 'I made the arrangement with your mother this morning, and...'

'Oh, no!' Amber gasped, suddenly realising that her mother was likely to appear on the scene any minute. 'I'm sorry—you can't *possibly* see around the house today. It's *absolutely* out of the question!' she babbled hysterically, glancing nervously behind her as she tried to close the door. 'I haven't yet told my mother, you see. She doesn't realise...she has no idea that the Hall is for sale. You'll just have to go away, and...and maybe come back some other time.'

Unfortunately, Max Warner had quickly taken a firm grip of the situation. Swiftly placing a well-shod foot in the door, he thanked Mr Glover for his services, smoothly informing the estate agent that he was quite capable of coping with the 'delicate' state of affairs at the Hall.

'There's no need to worry or disturb Mrs Grant. I'm quite confident that her daughter will be pleased to give me a personal conducted tour around the house.'

Oh, no, I won't! Amber screamed silently at him as the house agent gave a helpless shrug of his shoulders, walking back down the steps as Max pushed the door open, moving calmly past her trembling figure into the wide, spacious hall.

Completely stunned, Amber could only stare at him with glazed eyes, quite certain that she must be in the midst of some awful nightmare.

'I should have been in touch with you before now,' Max told her quietly. 'But I've been abroad and only recently heard the news.'

'"The news"?' she echoed blankly.

'I merely wanted to say that I was very sorry to learn about Clive's death.'

'Yes...um...it was a long time ago, of course. So much seems to have happened since then,' she muttered with a helpless shrug.

'However, it does seem as though you've done very well for yourself, Amber,' he drawled, glancing around at the old family portraits in their heavy gilt frames and the warm, comfortable effect of copper vases filled with greenery against the highly polished, old oak panelling.

The unexpectedly cynical, scathing note in his deep voice acted as a dash of freezing cold water on her shocked, numb state of mind. Her hackles rising, she was just about to demand an explanation for his sudden appearance—surely he couldn't really be interested in buying the house?—when her mother floated into the hall.

'How nice to see you. Have you come far?' Violet murmured, giving the tall man a welcoming smile.

Amber nearly groaned aloud. This was definitely *not* the time for her mother to be putting on a performance of her 'gracious hostess' routine!

Max took the older woman's outstretched hand and smiled warmly down at her. 'It's some time since we've met. However, I think that you'll probably remember my father, the Reverend Augustus Warner. He was the vicar here at Elmbridge some years ago.'

Violet beamed up at the man towering over her slight frame. 'Of course, I remember him. And you must be Max. The naughty boy who was always in trouble,' she added with a twinkling smile.

'Indeed I was!' he agreed with a grin.

'Well—you've certainly grown since those days! It looks as though you've done very well for yourself,' Violet told him, casting an approving glance over his expensive, obviously hand-tailored, dark grey suit.

'Now—I'm sure that you must have had a long drive.
How about a nice cup of tea?'

'Mother! I really don't think...'

'Nonsense, dear,' Violet murmured, ignoring her
daughter's husky, strangled protest as she placed a
hand on his arm, leading Max towards the large sitting
room. 'If he's driven some distance, I'm sure the poor
man must be simply dying of thirst.'

'*Mother*...!' Amber whispered urgently, but the
older woman clearly had no intention of taking any
notice of her desperate plea. As for the 'poor man'—
he merely turned his dark head to give her a cool,
sardonic smile before accompanying the older woman
into the sitting room.

Left standing alone in the hall, Amber could feel
her initial shock and dismay rapidly giving way to
long-suppressed feelings of rage and anger. How *dare*
Max swan back into her life, completely out of the
blue like this? Not only intimating that she'd married
poor Clive for his money, but with absolutely no appearance of regret—let alone an abject apology for
the way he'd treated her in the past.

However, just as she was telling herself fiercely that
she'd *never* sell the Hall to Max—not even if he offered her a million pounds—Amber caught sight of
herself in a large mirror hanging on the wall.

Nearly fainting with shock and dismay, it was all
she could do not to shriek out loud in horror! The
woman gazing back at her looked as though she'd
been drawn through a knot-hole backwards, her face
hot and flushed from the heat of the stove, and her
apron covered with smears of flour and mincemeat.

No wonder Max had been looking at her with such a caustic, scathing expression on his handsome face!

Realising that it was far too late to worry about his initial impression, Amber flew back along the corridor into the kitchen. Slinging the kettle on the hot plate of the ancient Aga, and practically throwing a tea tray of cups and saucers together, she ran back to the hall and up the wide curving staircase, taking the steps two at a time as she raced towards her bedroom.

Now, when it was almost too late, the shock waves of Max's unexpected arrival were gradually clearing from her mind. And it was the sharp, sudden awareness of the fresh danger she was facing that lent wings to her feet as she hastily stripped off the grubby, sticky apron and ran into the adjoining bathroom to wash her hands and face. Dragging a brush through her tangled hair, she could feel her heart pounding like a sledgehammer, just as if she'd been doing an exhausting aerobics workout. And it looked as if she was going to need all the agility of just such an exercise, she told herself breathlessly as she desperately tried to pull herself together.

Unless she could put a gag on her mother's garrulous tongue, there was a strong possibility that she was going to find herself in the middle of an utterly *disastrous* situation. The only chink of blue in an otherwise dark, ominous cloud was that she could hear the faint sounds of footsteps and movement overhead—evidence that Lucy and Emily were still playing happily together up in the attic.

Fervently praying that the little girls would stay safely out of sight, Amber quickly checked her appearance in a large, full-length mirror. Unfortunately, there was nothing she could do about her old navy sweater and jeans. Mostly because she couldn't spare the time, but also because she was determined not to let Max think that his sudden, startling manifestation on her doorstep mattered a jot to her one way or another.

Who are you trying to fool? she asked herself with disgust, realising that there was little she could do to disguise the hectic flush on her pale cheeks, or the hunted, wary look in her nervous green eyes. There was nothing for it, but to face the music. Let's hope they're playing my tune, she thought hysterically, her stomach churning with nerves as she quickly left the room.

'Max and I have just been reminiscing about old times,' her mother trilled happily as Amber entered the sitting room carrying the tea tray. 'We really do miss his dear father, don't we?'

'Er... yes, we do,' Amber muttered, trying to stop her hands from shaking as she poured the tea. Carefully avoiding Max's eyes, she chose a seat on the other side of the room, as far away from him as possible.

She'd been very fond of the Reverend Warner, a rather austere and scholarly widower, who'd been the vicar of Elmbridge during the years when she had been growing up. However, it had been obvious that neither he nor the rapid succession of housekeepers at the vicarage had the first notion of how to cope with his motherless son, Max—who'd gained a considerable local reputation as a wild tearaway.

'You'll hardly recognise the town nowadays,' Violet informed him. 'The old Victorian theatre has been turned into a multiple cinema, and there's a hideous new supermarket next to the railway station,' she added, oblivious of her daughter's tense figure as she turned to ask, 'What do they call it, dear?'

'Pick 'n' Pay,' Amber muttered, staring fixedly down at the cup in her trembling hands.

This is absolutely ridiculous! What *am* I doing, making polite conversation as if I've never met this man before...? she asked herself with mounting hysteria, convinced that she'd somehow strayed into a completely mad, unreal world. And why was Max here? Surely he couldn't be seriously interested in buying the Hall—not when Sally had said he was based in London?

For the first time since she'd clapped eyes on him, Amber realised that she knew nothing about Max—or what had happened to him during the past eight years. But obviously, such an attractive man was bound to be married by now, she told herself grimly.

'...isn't that right, dear?'

'What?' Jerked out of her depressing thoughts, Amber gazed at her mother in confusion.

'I was just talking about some of your old friends who are still living in the town,' the older woman murmured, frowning in puzzlement at her daughter, who for some reason was looking strangely pale and nervous, before turning back to their visitor. 'There's Rose Thomas, of course. As it happens, Rose's daughter, Emily, is playing here with Lucy this afternoon, and...'

'I'm sure Max would like another cup of tea,' Amber said quickly.

'No, I'm fine, thank you,' he drawled, lifting the cup to his lips.

Luckily, it seemed as though her swift, hasty interruption had succeeded in turning her mother's thoughts in a new direction as she asked, 'Are you now thinking of coming back to live here in Elmbridge?'

'Well...' he murmured, pausing for a moment as he turned his dark head to gaze at her daughter's suddenly stiff, rigid figure. 'John Fraser and I are still trying to sort out the affairs of my grandmother, who died over a year ago. Unfortunately, following the fire, there's no longer a large house on the estate. So, I'm not entirely sure about my future plans.'

Violet Grant looked at him blankly for a moment before exclaiming, 'Goodness me! I'd quite forgotten that old Lady Parker was your grandmother. She must have been well over ninety.'

'Ninety-two, I believe,' he agreed with a dry smile.

'I hadn't seen anything of her for the past ten years. But it was a shock to hear that she'd died in that terrible fire,' she told him sorrowfully. 'Such a lovely house—what a shame that it's now nothing but a burnt-out ruin. Is it *really* true that Lady Parker cut your mother off without a penny?' Violet added, unable to resist a juicy piece of gossip. 'That she refused to either see or speak to her daughter after she ran away to marry your father?'

Max shrugged his broad shoulders. 'Who knows? I certainly never met my grandmother,' he said briefly,

before changing the subject and encouraging the older
woman to relate all the changes that had taken place
in the town over the past few years.

Once her mother was launched upon the safe,
harmless topic of the recent development of
Elmbridge, Amber could feel some of her nervous
tension draining away. And it gave her a chance to
covertly study the man she hadn't seen for such a long
time.

Although they'd grown up together, the six-year
difference in their ages had seemed the most enormous
gap when she'd first entered her teens. Especially as
Max had always appeared to be older and more mature
than his true age. There had been something about
the determined set of his mouth and the glittering blue
eyes that had never been young. And, while she'd been
too dazed by his sudden reappearance to register more
than an instant recognition, she was now able to see
that Max appeared to have hardly changed at all.

Although that wasn't strictly true, of course. There
was now an austere, almost stern cast to the youthful
features she had once known and an unfamiliar bleak
and steely glint in his startlingly clear blue eyes.
However, it seemed so unfair that, in all other re-
spects, he should still appear to be the same devastatingly attractive man that she remembered only too
well.

And then, as he shifted slightly in his seat, the
movement of his broad shoulder and the quick,
fleeting smile with which he greeted something her
mother was saying to him sent a sudden sharp quiver
of sexual awareness rippling through her body.

Gritting her teeth, Amber desperately tried to think of something—anything—to prevent herself from recalling the firmly muscled chest, slim hips and hard thighs lying beneath the dark formal suit he was wearing with such effortless poise and assurance.

Maybe it was a sense of the total injustice of life that lent an extra sharpness to her voice as she found herself saying, 'It's been very nice to see you again, Max. However, I'm sure you must be a busy man, and we really shouldn't take up any more of your valuable time.'

'Really, Amber!' her mother protested with a quick, nervous laugh as her daughter glanced pointedly down at her watch. 'Besides,' she added with a puzzled frown, 'surely dear Max is staying the night with us?'

'Nonsense!' Amber snapped, feeling as though her temper—already on a very short fuse—was about to erupt at any moment. 'Of course he isn't. He...er...he just happened to be in the area, and...'

'No, dear, you're quite wrong. Because, now I come to think about it, it must have been Max's name, which I wrote down this morning.'

'*What*?' Amber's green eyes widened in horror as the older woman vigorously nodded her head. 'But I checked on the note pad in the hall, and there's nothing there—only something about a call from the grocer.'

Violet Grant gave her daughter a slightly guilty, shamefaced smile. 'Yes, well...it looks as if I might have made a slight error,' she admitted airily. 'But I thought the man mentioned Mr Warnock. So, I naturally assumed it was something to do with our local grocer. I didn't realise the call was about Max Warner wanting to spend the night with us.'

You idiot—he's only here to view the house! Amber wanted to scream at her mother. But she couldn't. Not when she hadn't yet told the older woman about the proposed sale of the Hall. Oh, Lord! What on earth was she going to do about this increasingly perilous situation?

Unfortunately, Violet Grant—now with the bit firmly between her teeth—appeared to be virtually unstoppable.

'It will be so nice having an old friend staying here with us, here at the Hall,' she told Max. 'I still haven't got used to complete strangers marching through the house. Although our paying guests always say that it's so much nicer and more comfortable than an impersonal hotel,' she confided before turning to Amber. 'There's no problem, dear. After all, we have plenty of rooms available.'

Amber knew that she ought to be thoroughly ashamed of a sudden, overwhelming urge to place her clenched hands tightly about her mother's neck. 'We're ... um ... we're all booked up,' she lied wildly.

'How can we be?' Violet frowned. 'Only this morning, you were saying that you wished we had some guests for the weekend.'

Amber gritted her teeth. She was just trying to think of some of their regular visitors, who might have arranged to stay at very little notice, when she caught sight of the chilly, mocking gleam in Max's glittering blue eyes.

Her heart sank like a stone as she suddenly realised that he was actually enjoying her discomfiture. Although, what she'd done to deserve his enmity, she had no idea. After all, *he* was the one who'd abandoned her.

'I'd be delighted to stay here at the Hall,' Max drawled, his mouth twisting with sardonic amusement at the expression of consternation and dismay clearly visible on Amber's face. 'Unfortunately...' he added after a long pause, 'I have to return to London tonight. But I'd be very interested to see over this house.' He turned to smile at Violet. 'I understand that it dates from Tudor times, and is one of the oldest houses in Elmbridge.'

The older woman nodded her head. 'Yes, you're quite right, it is. I'm sure Amber would be delighted to show you around.'

Oh, God—he's positively enjoying this! Amber realised, her body almost shaking with tension. Far from being prepared to accept that he wasn't wanted, Max was clearly getting the maximum amount of grim enjoyment from this fraught situation. And time was running out. She *had* to get rid of him—as quickly as possible. But how on earth was she going to do it?

Just as she was coming to the conclusion that the sooner she showed him around the house—keeping well away from the attic, of course—the sooner he'd be gone, her desperate thoughts were interrupted by a loud knock.

'Hello...?' Rose Thomas put her head around the sitting-room door. 'I've just come to fetch Emily. I hope she's been behaving herself?'

'Of course she has.' Amber turned to smile at her friend, momentarily overcome with relief and euphoria at the welcome interruption. But, as she heard the sound of childish laughter only a second or two later, she realised there was nothing she could do to avoid a catastrophic disaster.

'Mummy...Mummy! We've had a really *stupendous* time dressing up in Granny's old clothes!' Lucy called out as she ran full tilt into the sitting room, quickly followed by Emily. 'We looked absolutely *terrific*!'

'I'm sure you did,' Amber managed to gasp, almost frozen with terror as she watched the little girls running excitedly around the room. She had no hope of being able to fool a clever, perceptive man like Max. But Rose, who'd known Lucy since she was a baby...? Would she notice the startling similarity between the two heads of dark, curly hair and sparkling blue eyes?

But her friend clearly hadn't noted anything amiss as she gazed across the room at the tall, dark stranger who was rising to his feet.

'Surely, it can't be...?' Rose exclaimed as the man gave her a broad smile. 'Good Heavens—it really *is* Max Warner!' she laughed, her cheeks pink with excitement as he crossed the room towards her. 'I'd heard that you were now back in the country, but never expected to see you quite so soon. You hardly seem to have changed at all.'

'Since I shudder at the memory of myself as a wild teenager, I sincerely hope that I have, my dear Rose,' Max grinned, taking her hand and lifting it gallantly to his lips.

Despite her fright and panic, Amber felt a flash of indignation at this piece of quite outrageous flattery. Surely plain, calm, sensible Rose *couldn't* be so silly as to fall for such a line? However, as they chattered together, with her friend sparkling beneath the awful man's quite overwhelming charm, it really did seem as if she'd become momentarily transformed into a lovely woman.

You had to hand it to Max—he was a real con artist! she acknowledged grimly as Rose very reluctantly took her leave.

'*Well*...!' she exclaimed as Amber accompanied her and Emily across the hall towards the front door. 'When I arrived and saw that glamorous car, it never occurred to me that it might be Max Warner. What a surprise!'

'Yes, it certainly is,' Amber agreed bleakly.

'I don't understand.' Rose frowned. 'If you weren't expecting him—what on earth is he doing here?'

'Don't ask!' she groaned. 'It's all to do with the sale of the house. But everything has become so complicated——' Amber broke off, looking nervously back over her shoulder. 'I... I'll give you a ring tomorrow...explain everything,' she added, quickly bending down to kiss Emily goodbye, before dashing swiftly back to the sitting room.

Unfortunately, on her return, she discovered that even those few minutes' absence had proved to be fatal.

'...of course, Lucy's a very clever little girl,' her mother was saying. 'I'm hoping that she'll be clever enough to get into the local grammar school. But, as

she's only seven years old, there's still a few years to
go yet,' she added, smiling she patted the glossy, dark
curls of the child sitting on her lap.

'But I'm going to be eight years old in June,' Lucy
added quickly, jumping to her feet and running over
to the tall man leaning elegantly against the mantelpiece. 'How old are you?'

'I'm as old as my face—and just a little older than
my teeth,' Max retorted, waving aside her grandmother's protest as he smiled idly down at the small
girl.

'That's a *very* clever answer!' Lucy grinned up at
the man towering over her small figure. 'Are you going
to be staying with us for a while?'

'I'm afraid not,' he murmured, his dark brows
creasing into a puzzled frown as he gazed down at the
little girl.

'That's a pity, because I really like riddles. My
friend, Emily, told me a new one today—and I bet
Granny won't know the answer,' she confided, before
turning to skip back across the carpet to where Violet
was sitting. 'When is a pony not a pony?'

The older woman smiled and shook her head.

'When it's turned into a field!' Lucy shouted before
collapsing into a fit of giggles.

Standing frozen in the open doorway, Amber felt
as if she were viewing the curtain rise on the last act
of a Greek tragedy. Numbly waiting for nemesis to
strike, she watched as Max turned his head to look
into the large mirror over the mantelpiece. She saw
his body becoming taut and rigid, his eyes narrowing
to dark points of hard steel as he stared first at himself,

and then at the reflection of the small girl on the other side of the room.

Paralysed by panic, and helplessly unable to prevent her whole world from crashing down about her head, Amber's heart thumped wildly in her chest as Max continued to stare blindly into the mirror, his expression grim and forbidding. And then, as if coming to a decision, he turned to cross the room. Murmuring a polite farewell to Violet Grant, he glanced down intently at Lucy for a moment, before striding swiftly towards where she stood in the doorway. Grasping Amber's arm in an iron grip, he barely halted his swift progress as he dragged her after him into the hall, then slammed the door shut behind them.

'*My God!*' he exploded, the sound of his angry voice reverberating loudly in the large, vaulted space of the hall. '*Why* didn't you tell me?'

'Tell you what?' she muttered, helplessly aware that she'd never been any good at telling lies as she felt the hot colour flooding over her pale cheeks. 'I . . . I don't know what you're talking about.'

'Oh, yes, you damn well do!' he retorted harshly, his fingers tightening cruelly on her arm. 'That little girl is obviously *my daughter*—for Heaven's sake!'

'No! No, you're quite . . . er . . . quite wrong. . . .' she whispered, desperately tried to evade his fierce gaze.

'I'm not prepared to listen to any stupid lies, Amber,' he ground out threateningly, before swearing violently under his breath as he glanced down at the slim gold watch on his wrist. 'Unfortunately, I'm already late for another appointment. But if you thought you'd seen the last of me eight years ago—

you were *very* much mistaken!' he growled, the icy-cold menace in his voice sending shivers of fright and terror running down her spine. 'Because, I'll be back just as soon as I can. And that's not a threat—it's a *promise*!'

And she had absolutely no doubt that he would be back, Amber told herself, shivering with cold and nervous exhaustion. Max had very clearly stated his firm intention of seeking her out once again. And there was *nothing* she could do, but wait with ever-mounting despair for his return.

It had seemed, during the past two weeks, as though she was existing in the midst of a living nightmare, never knowing from one moment to the next when or how he would turn up to cast an evil shadow over her life. And while she was normally very busy at this time of year, she'd hardly been able to concentrate on even the simplest task. In fact, with Max's sudden reappearance in her life, she was finding it almost impossible to focus on the present when her mind was so completely filled with memories of the past.

'Mummy...? Where are you?'

'Over here,' Amber called out as her small daughter appeared on the other side of the old walled garden.

'Do hurry up!' Lucy begged, running down the gravel path towards her. 'If we don't go soon, I'll miss my riding lesson.'

Amber grimaced as she glanced down at her watch. 'Sorry, darling, I completely forgot the time.'

'I hope you're going to change out of those old clothes,' Lucy told her, critically viewing her mother's slim figure, clothed in a scruffy pair of jeans beneath a windproof jacket, which had clearly seen better days. 'And you've got some leaves stuck in your hair.'

'Hey—relax! It's Saturday, remember? No one has to get all dressed up at the weekend,' Amber laughed, bending down to allow the little girl to remove the greenery from her thick, golden brown hair.

'I thought you were going to do some Christmas shopping.'

'Oh, yes, you're right. I'd completely forgotten. OK, you win,' she grinned through her hair at her daughter. 'I'll try and find something smarter to wear.'

A self-appointed arbiter of her mother's wardrobe, Lucy had very strong views on what was, and what wasn't, suitable attire for various social functions. However, not having any spare money to spend on clothes, Amber had quite cheerfully stopped worrying about the dictates of fashion a long time ago.

'What *are* you going to wear?' Lucy demanded as she finished removing the straw from her mother's hair.

'Oh, I'll think of something.'

'All my friends say that you're very pretty. When I'm grown up, I'm going to buy you lots and lots of lovely clothes,' Lucy told her solemnly.

'Thank you, darling!' Amber grinned down at her daughter. Although she was only twenty-six and still— if Philip Jackson was to be believed—an attractive woman, she knew that she'd never been half as pretty as Lucy. With her cloud of black curly hair and large, clear blue eyes, the little girl was the spitting image of her father. Which was yet another problem to be faced. Because it wasn't *just* the threat of Max's return that was causing her so much anxiety and distress—there was the added worry of how and when to break the news to her friends. And that was something she was going to have to do sooner rather than later. Because, while Rose had been far too excited by Max's sudden reappearance to notice the startling resemblance between father and daughter, Amber knew that she couldn't rely on her other friends being so blind. And, most important of all—what about Lucy herself? How on earth could she even begin to try and explain to such a young girl the torturous events of the past...?

'Oh, do stop day-dreaming, Mummy. *Please* hurry up!' Lucy pleaded, almost dancing with impatience.

'Just give me five minutes to change, and I'll be right with you,' Amber promised, sighing heavily as she picked up the basket full of vegetables before slowly following her daughter back down the garden path.

CHAPTER THREE

'DON'T panic—there are *still* ten shopping days to go before Christmas!'

Momentarily unnerved by the words being hoarsely whispered in her ear, Amber gave a startled yelp, nearly dropping her heavy load of parcels as she spun around to find herself staring up into the twinkling brown eyes of Philip Jackson.

'For Heaven's sake!' she gasped as the young doctor swiftly removed the packages from her arms. 'It's bad enough having to fight one's way through the crowds without you scaring me half to death!'

'I didn't mean to give you a fright,' he grinned. 'But why does everyone seem to be gripped by a "shop till you drop" frenzy at this time of year?'

'I don't know. It's crazy, isn't it?' she agreed as they walked slowly up the street. 'So, just what are *you* doing here, in the middle of town on a Friday morning?' she teased. 'Surely a busy doctor ought to be in his surgery looking after the sick and infirm.'

'I've taken the morning off for some last-minute shopping,' he confessed with a rueful grin, before insisting on leading her into the Market Tavern for a mug of their famous 'Winter Warmer'—hot chocolate with a dash of brandy. 'It will do you good, and you'll still be quite sober enough to drive home,' he assured her when she expressed her doubts about the wisdom of drinking in the middle of the day. 'On the other hand—how about joining me for lunch in one of the local restaurants?'

Amber shook her head. 'I'm sorry, Philip. I can't make it today. Mother's in bed with a heavy cold, and I must get back to keep an eye on her.'

'I'm sorry to hear that. Although I have to say that you don't look too well, either,' the doctor added, glancing with concern at her pale, finely drawn features and the dark shadows beneath her eyes.

'I'm all right,' she shrugged, perfectly well aware— from a despairing glance in her mirror this morning— that she was looking like death warmed up. Just as she knew that part of her present exhausted state of mind wasn't just the worry about Max's return. She was also becoming deeply disturbed about her mother.

Amber had finally been forced to explain to her mother the necessity of selling their home, and Violet Grant's reaction had been every bit as bad as she had feared. Amber still shuddered to recall the wild, hysterical accusations and virtual collapse of the older woman. It was well over a week since her mother had taken to her bed, claiming that she had a bad cold and refusing to leave her room—an action that was now causing her daughter grave concern.

Unfortunately, it was all too reminiscent of Violet's behaviour eight years ago, following the scandal and collapse of her husband's business. And so, while she was trying hard not to overreact to the situation, Amber knew that if her mother continued to avoid facing up to life by hiding in her bedroom, she was going to have to seek some serious medical advice.

'Would you like me to call and have a look at your mother?' Philip asked.

'No... er... not just at the moment—but I'll be in touch with you if she gets any worse,' Amber assured him before quickly changing the subject. 'What are you doing for Christmas? Are you still planning to join your family in Cumberland?'

He nodded. 'I only wish that you and Lucy were coming, too. My parents were really disappointed that you couldn't make it.'

'I'm sorry—but this is always such a busy time of the year for me,' she murmured evasively.

She was very fond of Philip and she also liked his mother and father whom she'd met when they'd visited their son earlier in the year. However, until finally making up her mind about whether to accept his many proposals of marriage, Amber hadn't wanted to become too involved with his family.

In any case, the idea of marrying *anyone* was just about the last thing on her mind at the moment. Besides, it would be totally unfair to involve the young doctor in a nasty local scandal, which was likely to erupt just as soon as Max Warner carried out his threat to return.

It was now three weeks since she'd seen Max, and she still didn't feel able to relax. It was like waiting for a bomb to go off, she told herself grimly, realising that there was no way out of the trap in which she now found herself. Because, even if Max only intended to visit the small town every now and then, it would be impossible to hide the truth. With her glossy black curls and large blue eyes, it was going to be glaringly obvious to all and sundry that Lucy was an absolute carbon copy of her father.

Amber knew that she couldn't put it off any longer. She *must* tell Rose and her other close friends before news of the whole story became public property. But finding the courage to do so seemed completely beyond her at the moment. Even trying to explain what had happened in the past to Philip, for instance—who, like everyone else in the town, believed Lucy to be Clive Stanhope's daughter—was enough to make her break out in a cold sweat.

'...so I'll pick you up at about seven o'clock. OK?'

'Hmm...?' Amber stared blankly up at her companion before realising that she'd been so immersed in her own dark, sombre thoughts that she hadn't heard a word he'd been saying.

Philip gazed at her with a wounded expression in his kind brown eyes. 'I thought we'd arranged, some weeks ago, to go to the buffet supper party in the old Assembly Rooms? I hear the organisers are hoping for a large turnout to raise funds and support the town's protest about the destruction of the old Tide Mill.'

'Oh, I'm sorry—I'd forgotten all about it,' she confessed with a tired, guilty smile. 'Mainly because I've been so busy trying to catch up with all the last-minute orders for Christmas cakes. And, with Lucy away until tomorrow, I've been working flat out in the kitchen,' she added, explaining that Rose Thomas had invited her daughter to join a family trip to London. 'They're staying the night with David Thomas's sister, and Lucy was absolutely ecstatic about the thought of seeing a pantomime *and* visiting a large department store to meet Santa Claus!'

'She'll have a wonderful time,' he agreed with a warm smile. 'But it's a pity Rose will miss the party. No one seems to know who owns the development company, Suffolk Construction. But their plans to pull down the old mill and build a large new marina in the old mill pond certainly seem to have upset just about everyone in the town. Feelings are running pretty high at the moment,' he added with a frown. 'I hope things will soon calm down.'

'So do I,' she agreed, aware that most people in the town were extremely angry and grimly determined to keep the modern developers at bay.

Standing derelict and unused for the past forty years, the ancient Tide Mill was a rare survivor of a bygone age. Unfortunately, both the rapidly expanding tourist trade in the small East Anglian town and the increasingly loud demands for a modern marina by the local sailing fraternity had led to the threatened destruction of this important landmark in the town.

The local outcry against the loss of the mill was mainly due to its ancient, almost unique system of operation. Since it had depended on the river water being trapped in the mill pond at high tide, which was then released to turn the huge wheels when the tide had fallen, the old mill's working hours had been dictated solely by the flow of tidal water entering the river from the North Sea.

As far as Amber knew, there was only one other such mill, farther up the river at Woodbridge, which had been saved from decay some twenty years ago. 'If the inhabitants of that town could raise the money to restore *their* mill, so can *we!*' Rose Thomas had declared stoutly, before quickly calling on the help of her friends and organising strong local resistance to the plans for its demolition.

It was at this point that Amber had found herself in an embarrassing position. Because, the old mill, with its surrounding land and large mill pond, had once been owned by the Stanhope family, who'd leased the property to a succession of millers ever since the sixteenth century. Unfortunately, it was her late husband, Clive, needing money to settle some gambling debts, who had sold the mill to a local builder some time ago.

'Nobody blames you,' Rose had repeatedly assured her, pointing out that it was hardly Amber's fault if the land had changed hands several times over the past few years. 'After all, there's a world of difference between building a few houses on the site— and Suffolk Construction's plans for a glitzy, modern marina!'

If only there was some way to satisfy the yachtsmen without having to destroy such an ancient building, Amber told herself, gathering up her parcels as her companion paid for their drinks. The obvious answer, of course, was to talk the matter over with Suffolk Construction. But, as Philip had pointed out, nobody knew anything about either the development company or its owners.

'Is anything troubling you, Amber?' he asked, noting her shivering with cold as they left the warmth and comfort of the Market Tavern. 'You don't look at all well.'

'I'm perfectly all right. Really, I am,' she told him firmly as he continued to gaze at her with a worried frown. 'I'm just feeling a bit tired, that's all. But I'm quite well enough to attend tonight's party.'

'Well, for goodness' sake, try to make sure you eat properly and get some decent night's sleep. Otherwise, I'm going to insist on taking you down to the surgery for a complete overhaul.'

'OK, OK, anything you say, Doctor,' she grinned, raising a hand in mock surrender.

'By the way, I was very sorry to hear that you've decided to sell the Hall,' he said as they slowly made their way along the High Street, which was thronged with Christmas shoppers. 'David Thomas told me that you're letting him have a look at the old house deeds.'

'Yes . . .' she muttered, feeling guilty at having been so busy that she'd completely forgotten to tell Philip about the forthcoming sale. 'I've lent the huge pile of old documents to David because he's so interested in local history.'

'I wish you didn't have to sell your home,' he told her with a frown. 'You know how I feel about you, Amber. And, although this isn't either the time or the place, you must let me know if there's anything I can do.'

'Yes...yes, of course I will,' she murmured, grateful to be saved from having to say any more as they were momentarily parted by the many passers-by crowding the pavement.

The news that the Hall was now up for sale had obviously become a topic of conversation in Elmbridge. In fact, Amber had been surprised by the amount of people who'd stopped her in the street today, all expressing their regret and sympathy at the loss of her home. Despite all her problems, it was really comforting to know that so many inhabitants of this small provincial town seemed to be genuinely concerned for both her and her family's welfare.

Rose, Sally and her other friends had rallied around, promising to try and find a small cottage to house the family. Unfortunately, there didn't seem to be anything at all suitable on the market at the moment. But as 'Gloomy Glover', the house agent, had so bluntly pointed out, there was no need for her to worry about that, since it was likely to take her some time before she found a buyer for her present home.

'I had hoped that Mr Warner might be interested,' he'd told her before giving a mournful shake of his head. 'But why would a single man—however wealthy he might be—want to saddle himself with such a huge old house? No,' he'd added with a heavy sigh, 'I'm afraid that it will take me a long time to find a buyer for your property, Mrs Stanhope. A very long time indeed.'

Amber hadn't known exactly *what* she felt on learning that Max wasn't a married man. However, the news of his brief visit to Elmbridge—and that he apparently had neither a wife or children—had become a major talking point amongst her friends. Rose, for instance, had been clearly thrilled to meet him again, as well as being highly amused by Sally

Fraser's groans of envy at having missed the opportunity to do so.

'If *only* I hadn't been out when he called to see John! Was he really every bit as handsome as he used to be?' Sally had demanded, almost grinding her teeth with frustration as Rose pretended to give the matter some thought.

'Well...' she'd winked at Amber before turning to give Sally a bland smile, 'on the whole, I think that Max is definitely *more* attractive nowadays. He's still very good-looking, of course. But now that he's become such an obviously sophisticated and successful man, he seems somehow more...er...more sexy—if you know what I mean?'

'Oh, *why* didn't I have the luck to meet him?' Sally wailed before rushing off to spread the news of the handsome prodigal's return.

'Don't say it—I know that I ought to be ashamed of myself!' Rose had laughingly confessed to Amber when they were left alone together. 'But it isn't often that I manage to upstage Sally. And, although *you* don't seem to be very struck by Max Warner, I really must admit—happily married woman that I am—that he definitely made me feel quite weak at the knees!'

Amber, who dearly wished that she'd taken her house deeds to David Thomas's office instead of deciding to leave them with Rose, could only give her friend a weak, sickly smile before rapidly changing the subject.

'Here we are.'

'Hmm...?' she blinked, before realising that she was standing beside her old Land Rover.

'You really should lock your car when you leave it parked in the street like this,' Philip told her sternly as he opened the door and put her parcels on the back seat.

'The locks are useless—they're all rusted away, and I can't afford to fit any new ones,' she explained with a brief, helpless shrug of her shoulders. 'Thank you for that lovely, warming drink—and for carrying my shopping all this way,' she added as he bent down to give her a quick kiss on the cheek before striding off down the street.

Settling down into the driving seat, she turned on the ignition—only to be met by complete silence. Some moments later, having tried everything she knew to try and start her vehicle, Amber gave a deep heartfelt groan before beginning to swear violently under her breath.

'This old wreck should have been thrown on the scrap heap years ago!'

The sound of the deep voice caused Amber, for the second time that day, to give a startled shriek of fright and alarm. Quickly turning her head, she found herself facing the tall, dark-haired man who'd dominated her dreams for the past few weeks.

'*Max*! What on earth are you doing here?' Amber gasped, her face as white as a sheet as she stared glassy-eyed at the tall figure, whose perfectly tailored, black cashmere coat over a sober dark grey suit seemed more appropriate for the City of London than the small market town of Elmbridge.

'It would appear that I am about to have the pleasure of rescuing a damsel in distress,' he drawled coolly.

'Not *this* damsel you aren't!' she snapped nervously.

'Don't be tiresome, Amber. This heap of rust clearly isn't going anywhere. However, since I was on my way to Elmbridge Hall, I'll be able to give you a lift home.' He nodded towards the long black sports car parked beside the pavement a few feet away from the Land Rover.

'Why are you doing this to me?' she wailed, thumping her steering wheel with an angry fist.

'Doing what?' Max gave a harsh, sardonic bark of laughter. 'Is it *my* fault that you're driving around in an ancient vehicle, which should have gone to the great scrapyard in the sky years ago?'

'I meant why...why *here*...in the middle of the High Street?' she ground out through clenched teeth. 'Why couldn't you just telephone and make an appointment to see me? Like any perfectly normal, sane person?'

'Because I became fed up with getting nothing but your damned answerphone,' he retorted, taking no notice of her furious protests as he swiftly transferred her parcels and bags of shopping to his vehicle. 'Jump in—and shut up!' he added grimly, waiting with barely concealed impatience until she did as she was told.

However, Amber had no intention of obeying his last command.

'If you rang when my answerphone was switched on,' she said furiously as the long, low sports car snaked along the country lanes to Elmbridge Hall, 'I

can see no reason why you couldn't leave a sensible
message like everyone else.'

'If I remember correctly, you run a boarding-
house....'

'I most certainly do not! We take in paying guests,'
she snapped before realising—with a sinking heart—
that she was beginning to sound just like her mother.

'...and I have no intention of allowing complete
strangers to listen to my private phone calls,' he told
her firmly. 'Incidentally, I don't think much of the
prissy message you've put on the machine. Quite
frankly, Amber,' he added, his mouth twitching with
amusement, 'you sounded like a frightened rabbit!'

'Thank you!' she ground out, furious at the description of her voice—and also with herself for having
been so easily outmanoeuvred.

When a friend had offered her a very cheap, second-
hand telephone answering system some weeks ago, it
had seemed like a gift from heaven. Not only would
it cope with her mother's complete inability to take
down a simple message, but she'd also hoped that it
would help her to avoid any direct contact with Max.
So that, when he left a message giving the date and
hour of his return, she wouldn't be taken unawares.
It had *never* occurred to her that he would refuse to
use the damn machine. Didn't he believe in modern
technology, or what?

'That's still no excuse for not contacting me in the
normal way,' Amber retorted bitterly. 'There was absolutely no need to...to kidnap me like this.'

'Kidnap? Surely I'm doing nothing more than rescuing you from an unfortunate predicament?' he

drawled smoothly before taking a hand off the wheel to punch some numbers into his car phone.

'I didn't *need* rescuing,' she ground out through gritted teeth. 'I could easily have sorted out the problem myself.'

'I very much doubt it,' Max murmured dryly, forestalling her angry retort as he picked up the phone.

'Ah, Cruickshank—it's Max Warner here. I want you to ring up the local garage and get them to pick up an ancient Land Rover, which has broken down in the High Street. Tell them to give it a thorough overhaul. Oh, there is just one thing,' he added. 'Please ask them to check the electrical wiring under the dashboard.'

'Oh, great!' Amber exploded at the end of his call. 'And just *what* am I supposed to use for transport while my car's being fixed?'

'I'll see that it's returned to you before I leave.'

She gave a shrill, angry laugh. 'If you think that amount of work can be done in the twinkling of an eye, you must be off your head! I've never heard of Mr Cruickshank, but while our local garage is fairly efficient, they can't perform miracles!'

As the harsh, grating tones of her normally soft voice seemed to echo loudly within the confines of the car, Amber forced herself to take a deep breath and try to calm down. Shouting her head off or making cutting remarks wasn't going to get her anywhere with this obviously hard-boiled, tough man.

'Just what are you doing here in Elmbridge anyway?' she asked a few moments later in a quieter tone of voice.

But, even as she said the words, Amber knew that it was a stupid question. Because, of course, she already knew the answer. However, she was surprised to find, after all the unrelenting stress of the past three weeks, that it was almost a relief to be at last facing the man who'd caused her such overwhelming fear and tension.

She was well aware that it was extremely childish to be so rude and aggressive, or to keep on quarrelling so furiously with Max. But, driven as she was by an almost overwhelming need to hurt and wound him as much as possible, it was also extraordinarily liberating to be able to release some of the long-suppressed, pent-up rage and fury at the way he'd treated her in the past.

'Why am I here...?' He gave a nonchalant shrug of his broad shoulders. 'Surely you can't have forgotten my promise to return?'

'You're quite right—I haven't!'

'In that case, you will be pleased to hear that I'm still interested in looking over your house,' he drawled, coolly ignoring her grim snort of disbelief. 'Particularly since I was able to see very little of the Hall when I called some weeks ago.'

'If you're *so* keen to view the house, why didn't you make an appointment with Mr Glover?'

'When I last visited your house, you were insisting—almost hysterically so, in fact—that Mr Glover should definitely *not* be involved. Do I take it that you have now changed your mind?'

'Yes…no…I mean, it's not a problem any more—
not now that my mother knows about the sale,' she
muttered defensively.

'I hope she wasn't too upset?'

'Well, she obviously isn't thrilled about the situation,' Amber retorted caustically before adding
quickly, 'I'm afraid there's no question of your seeing
her today. She's in bed with a heavy cold.'

'I'm sorry to hear that. I hope she gets better soon,'
he said as they turned into the driveway leading to
Elmbridge Hall. 'Do you have any guests staying with
you at the moment?'

'No, as a matter of fact we don't. Why do you ask?'
she demanded, turning to glare at his handsome
profile with distrust and suspicion.

'I merely wanted to be sure that I wouldn't be
causing you any trouble,' he replied smoothly.
'However, from what you say, it seems as if there's
no reason why you can't give me a guided tour of the
house, hmm?'

After staring at him grimly for a moment, Amber
gave a heavy sigh. 'I suppose not,' she muttered as
his car came to a halt outside the front door.

Amber knew that it was undoubtedly spineless of
her to cave in, despite being quite certain that Max
had no real interest in the house. But there seemed
no point in continuing to defy this seemingly indomitable man. It was obvious that he was just
amusing himself by playing a savage game of cat and
mouse, waiting until she was in a total state of nervous
exhaustion before pouncing on what he *really* wanted.

And there was no doubt of what that would be, she told herself, suddenly feeling sick with nerves.

However, by the time Max was helping to carry her parcels into the kitchen, she'd managed to partially pull herself together—even if she was finding it difficult to stop shivering, despite the warmth of the room. It was some comfort to realise that with Lucy safely away in London, there was no chance of Max seeing the little girl. And before her daughter returned tomorrow, she'd have plenty of time in which to come up with a plan of action. Although exactly *what* she was going to say or do would depend on Max, of course. But after having been in such a blue funk for the past three weeks, feebly waiting like a condemned woman for the noose to tighten about her neck, it was about time she started using her brain.

It was stupid to be so frightened of this man. She might not have seen him for the past eight years, but he couldn't have changed all that much, surely? Desperately trying to ignore the tight knot of apprehension lying like heavy lead deep in her stomach, she knew that she *must* try to take control of this dire situation.

But Max clearly had no intention of allowing her to gain the initiative.

'What a charming room,' he murmured, gazing around the warm kitchen, dominated by a massive old-fashioned oak dresser and a large, well-scrubbed pine table surrounded by comfortable old chairs. 'In fact, I already feel so much at home, that I think I'll stay here for a night or two.'

'*What*?'

'My dear Amber, there's no need to sound quite so surprised,' he drawled mockingly as she stared at him with glazed, horrified eyes. 'You told me yourself that you frequently have paying guests.'

'Yes . . . but . . .'

'And, since you also told me a few moments ago that you don't have anyone staying at the moment, I'm quite sure there must be plenty of room.'

'No...no...you can't possibly stay here,' she gasped breathlessly, floundering as she tried to think of a sufficiently good excuse. 'I mean, a single man, on his own . . . it really wouldn't be at all . . . er . . . at all suitable,' she added lamely, waving her hands helplessly in the air.

He raised a dark, sardonic eyebrow. 'Are you telling me that you've *never* had a man staying here on his own?'

'Well . . . um . . .' she faltered, her voice dying away beneath the intense, mocking gaze of his clear blue eyes.

'How sensible not to try and lie to me. Especially since you always were a shocking liar!' he grinned.

Amber stared blindly at the tall figure calmly removing his dark overcoat, her head beginning to pound with a dull, throbbing ache as she desperately tried to cope with the situation.

It really did look as if it was only a sudden, last-minute idea of Max's to stay here at the Hall. Could it be that he was just teasing her? Trying to pile on the pressure so that she'd weakly agree to whatever it was he wanted? If so . . . maybe it *would* be a good idea to show him around the house after all. At least it might give her an opportunity to try and persuade him to go away or stay in a local hotel.

'OK, I'll give you a quick guided tour of the house,' she said grimly, moving towards the door.

However, it soon transpired that her half-formed, confused and hazy ideas for getting rid of Max hadn't a chance of being realised that quickly. As soon as they entered the hall—and almost before she knew what was happening—he had disappeared briefly through the front door, removed an overnight case from his car, and returned to follow her reluctant figure up the wide oak staircase.

'I...I can't really believe that you want to stay here,' she muttered helplessly as she showed him into a guest-room.

'Can't you?' he murmured, placing his case on a nearby chair, and raising an ironic, quizzical dark eyebrow as he gazed about the room, whose delicate antique furniture, long red velvet curtains and large paintings in heavy gilt frames gave an impression of comfortable warmth and luxury.

'No. Just as I can't see any reason why you should want to buy this house,' she retorted, aware that she was sounding strained and brittle as she moved quickly past him to jerkily open one of the large, mullioned windows.

'Maybe now that my grandmother has left me her estate, I feel like settling down here in Elmbridge,' he drawled, strolling across the carpet towards her. 'And, since there is now no longer a house on the land, I might well need somewhere to live, hmm?'

It all sounded very reasonable, but Amber still
didn't entirely believe him. And the atmosphere between them suddenly seemed to become tense and
claustrophobic.

It had been different while she'd been quarrelling
with him in the car. But now, standing so close to his
tall, dominant figure, she was starkly aware of the
hard, almost aggressively male body beneath the ex-
pensively tailored dark suit. How could she have made
the mistake of thinking that he hadn't changed? Because this was no longer the youth of twenty-four,
with his whole life stretching out before him. Now,
as Max turned to gaze down at her with a formidable,
enigmatic gleam in his glittering blue eyes, she suddenly realised that she was facing a fully mature and
dauntingly powerful man. A man, she instinctively
realised, who could prove to be very dangerous indeed.

'If... um ... if you want to look around the house,
I'm afraid you're going to have to wait while I provide
lunch for my mother,' she told him nervously.

'Ah, yes. I *was* surprised when you appeared to
need—in this day and age!—the protection of a
chaperon,' he drawled blandly, his eyes gleaming with
unconcealed mockery. 'After all, with your mother
and daughter living in the house, I'm quite sure that
your reputation must be spotless!'

How *could* she have ever imagined that she'd once
been wildly in love with this really foul, sarcastic man?
Amber asked herself wildly, trying to inch past his tall
figure towards the safety of the door.

'My mother isn't at all well,' she muttered, dismayed to find him moving to block her retreat.

'And your daughter...?' he enquired silkily. But when she didn't reply, remaining stubbornly silent as she glared defiantly up at him, the atmosphere in the bedroom suddenly became tense and very frightening. His mouth tightened ominously, a muscle beating in his jaw as his eyes became hard chips of blue ice.

'Don't even *think* of trying to play games with me, Amber!' The harsh, grating anger in his voice cracked like a whiplash in the quiet, still room as his hands came down on her slim shoulders; the strong fingers tightened like cruel talons in her soft flesh, shaking her roughly as though she were a rag doll.

'Let me go!' she cried, gasping with pain as she desperately tried to escape his vicelike grip.

'Only when you understand that it's pointless to defy me!' he snarled, his voice heavy with menace. *'I want to see my daughter.'*

'You can't...' she gasped, prevented from saying any more as she found herself trapped within a fierce, iron-like embrace, roughly forced against his hard body, a hand firmly gripping her chin and forcing her head up towards him. She had only a brief, fleeting glimpse of the raging anger in his steely blue eyes before his mouth possessed her lips with harsh, deliberate intent.

The bruising, relentless pressure seemed unending, forcing her lips apart as her helpless protest became an inaudible moan. Twisting and wriggling as she might, there seemed nothing she could do to escape. And then, the hand pressing her so firmly towards him began slowly sliding down over the curves of her body, the punishing torture of his mouth subtly changing, becoming soft and tender as his lips moved sensuously over hers, arousing a response she was helpless to control.

A treacherous warmth invaded her trembling body pressed so closely to his hard, muscular thighs, the soft seduction of his lips and tongue having a disastrous effect on her long-dormant emotions. Bemused as she was by the burning heat flooding her mind and body, she was still capable of realising that he was deliberately using his undoubted sexual expertise as a weapon, callously forcing her to acknowledge his mastery of her emotions. But it was eight long, long years since a man had kissed her like this, and trapped in a dense mist of raging desire, she was helplessly unable to prevent her body from hungrily responding to the tide of passion sweeping through her veins.

It seemed an age before Max finally raised his dark head, looking down at her flushed cheeks as she slowly opened her eyes.

Mentally paralysed for a moment, she gazed up at him in confusion, dazed and bewildered by his assault on her long-dormant senses. But as the harsh, cold facts of life finally broke through the miasma in her stunned mind, she gave a horrified sob as she tore herself from his arms. Fighting to control her ragged breathing, she stared at him in utter consternation.

What *had* she been doing? Panting as if she'd just run a mile, and totally appalled to find herself still quivering with sexual hunger, Amber almost collapsed with shame. How *could* she still be attracted to a man who, not content with callously abandoning her all those years ago, was now clearly intent on asserting his parental rights to her daughter? There was only one possible conclusion: she must be stark, raving mad!

Max's face was taut and strained, pale beneath his tan, his blue eyes glittering like steel chips. And while he, too, appeared to be breathing roughly, he seemed to have no difficulty in finding his voice.

'That was a mistake—and not one I have any intention of repeating,' he told her grimly. 'At the risk of sounding tedious, I'll repeat what I said a few moments ago. I want to see my daughter.'

'Well, that's just too bad—because she's not here!' Amber retorted savagely.

A moment later, she could almost sense the blood draining from her face, suddenly feeling quite sick as she realised that she'd just made a really terrible, *terrible* mistake. Because, if she'd ever hoped to deny the fact that Max was Lucy's father, she had now thrown away any chance of doing so.

CHAPTER FOUR

How *could* she have been such a fool?

Practically throwing the bread tins into the hot stove and loudly slamming the oven door shut did nothing to soothe Amber's fury with herself at having been such an idiot.

There was little comfort to be gained in realising that it wasn't entirely her fault; she'd been so emotionally shattered by Max's kiss that she hadn't even known whether it was night or day—let alone been capable of withstanding a tough cross-examination. Unfortunately, once she'd made the colossal mistake of telling him that Lucy was away from home, there had been nothing she could do to repair the damage.

If only she could have taken refuge upstairs in the privacy of her own bedroom, giving way to tears of overwhelming rage and anger—both with Max and herself. Unfortunately, with her mother's lunch to prepare, she had no choice in the matter. But there seemed nothing she could do to stop her hands shaking, her knees knocking together like castanets as she recalled Max's swift stride over the faded bedroom carpet, his hard blue eyes staring intently down at her trembling figure.

It had been no contest. He hadn't even needed to raise his voice. Once she'd glimpsed the flush of anger beneath his tanned skin, a pulse beating in his formidable jawline and the cruel, tight-lipped expression on his face, she'd immediately caved in.

'I'm telling you the truth. I...I really wasn't lying,' she had assured him quickly, her eyes sliding nervously away from his hard, steely gaze. 'Lucy really *isn't* here at the moment.'

'I'm pleased to hear that you've decided to be sensible, and that there's at least one battle I won't have to fight,' he'd grated, his words accurately confirming her own dismayed thoughts. 'So, where exactly *is* my daughter?'

'She...she's in London, with Rose Thomas's family,' Amber had muttered helplessly, being forced to explain that Lucy wasn't due to arrive back home until tomorrow, before Max had allowed her to leave the room.

Leaning wearily against the warm stove, Amber desperately tried to pummel her mentally weary brain into some sort of clear, cohesive thought. But it seemed an almost impossible task. She couldn't seem to banish from her mind the images of Max's sensual mouth poised above her own, her body still quivering in response to the erotic seduction of his lips and hands.

Oh, help! What on earth was she going to do? she moaned silently, knowing that there was virtually no chance of her being able to stop Max seeing Lucy tomorrow. And then, what? Would he insist on telling the little girl that he was her father?

Almost whimpering at the thought of her small daughter's safe, secure world being smashed to pieces,

Amber knew that there was nothing she could do to prevent it happening. However, there was no evading the harsh fact that, having been without a father all her life, Lucy might well be thrilled to discover she was the daughter of such a handsome, successful man. A man who could easily, for instance, buy his child anything her heart desired—even the pony, which the little girl had been wistfully hankering after for the past two years.

However, according to Mr Glover, Max wasn't a married man. So, without an established family of his own, it seemed unlikely that he was seriously intending to drag Lucy away to live with him in London—or wherever he was living at the moment. Even if he attempted to do such a thing, she was certain that the law must be on her side. Surely no judge would agree to a child being torn away from her natural mother? But since his claim to be interested in buying this house was obviously a total red herring, she *must* try to work out exactly why Max was here and what he hoped to achieve.

Unfortunately, and however much Amber tried, she could only come to one conclusion. It looked as if Max not only wanted to see the little girl, but he was also going to tell Lucy that he was her real, long-lost father.

But that wasn't all. While Amber was ashamed to be so pathetically small-minded, she dreaded the thought of Lucy's illegitimacy becoming widely known. Even thinking about all the hullabaloo and juicy, scandalous gossip—which was bound to run like wildfire around the small town—was enough to make her feel faint and dizzy.

'Ah, there you are,' Max said, almost causing her to jump out of her skin with nerves as he silently entered the room. 'I was just wondering where you'd got to.'

'This kitchen is strictly off limits to paying guests,' she informed him stonily, noting that he'd removed his suit jacket and tie, and was now wearing a black, V-necked cashmere sweater over the open-necked shirt, whose white collar only seemed to emphasise his deep tan and the firm muscular cords of his strong neck.

'But that restriction hardly applies to me,' he drawled coolly. 'Especially since we've established the fact that I'm now practically one of the family.'

Amber glared at him, desperately clamping her lips together in an effort to suppress an extremely rude reply.

Life was so damned unfair! Surely, if there was *any* justice in the world, this wretched man would have come to a sticky end a long time ago. But it seemed her friend, Rose, had, alas, been quite right. Instead of succumbing to a richly deserved and malignant fate, he was now obviously very rich, highly successful— and even *more* devastatingly attractive than ever.

'I'm told that you're a wonderful cook,' he murmured, his eyes flicking over her slender figure before glancing at the large pan of soup bubbling on the stove. 'And I must say, that smells absolutely delicious,' he added, with such an engaging smile that her heart almost missed a heat.

'Get lost, you smooth bastard!' Amber muttered under her breath as she turned away, reaching up for an apron hanging beside the stove.

'What did you say?'

'Oh . . . er . . . nothing,' she mumbled, determinedly keeping her back to him, her face flushed with anger, and she mentally cursed her fumbling fingers, suddenly all thumbs as she attempted to tie the apron strings into a bow.

'What are you giving your mother for lunch?' he enquired, moving across the room to lean casually against the large oak dresser.

Amber shrugged, taking the bread out of the oven before placing a tray on the table. 'I can't think why you're interested. However, if you *must* know—my mother's having freshly baked bread with home-made leek and potato soup, followed by apple pie and cream. I *do* hope the menu meets with your approval?' she added sarcastically.

'It most certainly does. I hope you've got enough for me, too.'

'*What* . . .?'

'I had to leave London at the crack of dawn this morning. Which means that I haven't had a thing to eat all day.'

'Talk about damn cheek!' she gasped, almost unable to believe that she'd heard him correctly. 'First you kidnap me in broad daylight, then you invite yourself to stay in this house, assault me upstairs in the bedroom, and now . . .' She waved a wooden spoon wildly in the air. 'Now you're calmly expecting me to serve you lunch!'

'Come on, Amber!' he grinned wolfishly at her. 'That kiss was hardly what I would call an "assault". In fact, I was amazed to discover just how enthusiastically you responded to...'

'I did nothing of the sort!' she snapped furiously, her cheeks burning with embarrassment. 'I was just taken by surprise, that's all.'

'Oh, really?' he drawled, a clear note of disbelief in his voice, before adding firmly, 'I suggest that we both do our best to forget the whole unfortunate episode.'

'Yes... well, that seems a good idea,' she muttered, carefully avoiding his eye as she laid the cutlery on her mother's tray.

'However, I wasn't kidding,' he told her with a disarming smile. 'I really am extremely hungry.' When she remained stubbornly silent, he added plaintively, 'Surely you can't refuse to feed a starving man?'

'Oh, no? I wouldn't like to bet on it,' she retorted grimly.

You really had to hand it to Max, she told herself, not knowing whether to burst into tears or scream with hysterical laughter. His capacity for sheer, brass nerve was *totally* amazing! And since he was also clearly intending to make her present life as difficult as possible, this whole ghastly situation was rapidly becoming a complete farce.

Astonishingly, she found herself giving a dry, ironic bark of grim laughter. 'Oh... all right. I'll give you lunch. But only because at least one of us ought to behave like a civilised human being,' she told him coldly before carrying the tray upstairs to her mother.

Unfortunately, Violet Grant was feeling fretful, one minute saying that she wasn't hungry, and the next demanding to know why her daughter was late with her meal.

Determined not to let the older woman know about Max's visit—not too difficult, since her mother's rooms were in a separate wing at the side of the house—Amber was forced to spend some considerable time trying to calm her mother down and make her more comfortable. All to no avail.

'If only dear Clive were still alive. *He* would never have agreed to sell this house,' Violet muttered in a querulous tone of voice. 'Clive was such a kind, generous man. I hope you realise just how lucky you were to be married to him,' she added peevishly. 'Husbands like that don't grow on trees, you know.'

'No, I know they don't,' Amber agreed quietly, refusing to be drawn into a silly quarrel as she tried to coax the older woman to drink her soup.

While her mother's grouchy remarks were entirely out of character, and solely due to her acute depression about the sale of their house, she had to admit that Violet was right. Clive had indeed proved to be an exceptionally kind and generous husband. Not that she had ever dreamed of marrying him all those years ago when she'd been so madly in love with Max Warner.

Amber could still recall with remorseless clarity her feelings of overwhelming fear and panic when a London doctor had confirmed that she was expecting a baby. With the family house sold to pay her father's creditors and her mother still in hospital, she'd been staying with her aunt, who lived in a gloomy old house in Kensington. But urgently needing to earn some money to feed and clothe herself, she'd been lucky enough to find a temporary Christmas job in the Men's Gifts section of a world-famous department store.

It had been a long time before Amber forced herself to accept the hard, brutal truth that Max was never going to get in touch with her. And even longer to come to terms with the bitter pain and humiliation of his cruel desertion. Having always known about Max's wild reputation as a breaker of hearts, she knew that she had only herself to blame for having been so starry-eyed. So high on cloud nine, that while she'd given him her future address and phone number in London, she had no idea of where to contact him in America.

Where could she go? What *was* she going to do? Day after day, the questions seemed to pound away like sledgehammers in her brain. There was no way she could tell her aged spinster aunt about the baby. Nor could she bring herself to consider terminating the pregnancy. In fact, during her long working hours, it seemed as if she was merely existing on autopilot, smiling blankly at her customers while all the time her mind was in a ferment as she desperately tried to think of a solution to her problem. And then, one day, she found herself selling some cuff-links and a tie to an old friend from her·childhood.

The orphan grandson of a wealthy landowner, Clive Stanhope had been raised at Elmbridge Hall before being sent away to boarding-school on the death of his grandfather. Although Amber had only met him briefly since he'd inherited the Hall and its large estate, he seemed delighted to see her again, and insisted on taking her out to dinner.

Clive had proved to be a warm and amusing companion, managing to lift her dismal spirits by making her laugh. Discovering that they had many interests in common, he'd also been very kind and sympathetic about her father's death and her mother's hospitalisation. So much so, in fact, that she was astounded to find herself telling him about her pregnancy and her desperate worries about the future.

'There's a simple answer to that problem,' he'd told her cheerfully, tossing back a large glass of wine. 'The solution is to marry me—and we can then both live happily ever after!'

Convinced that he was joking, she'd laughed at such a ridiculous idea. But after listening to Clive's explanation of just how lonely he found his grandfather's huge old house, and his aimless existence, which seemed to revolve around drink and gambling, she found herself feeling very sorry for the supposedly lucky, rich young man.

'To tell the truth, Amber, I seem to have made a complete and utter mess of my life so far. But at least I've still got enough sense to know that I must try to pull myself together. And if I had someone like you by my side—someone to help turn that draughty old house into a home—I'm quite sure that I could straighten myself out.'

Despite her protests that she couldn't possibly agree to such a mad suggestion, Clive had pointed out that his proposal of marriage would solve many of her urgent problems. 'The only money you've got is what you can earn, right? So, what happens when the baby arrives? Will you give him or her up for adoption? Or are you planning to try to live on what little you can dig out of the Social Services? Because you only have to read the newspapers to know what a nightmare scenario that can be!

'And what about your mother?' he continued. 'She's not likely to be happy living in a small, cramped apartment—even if you could afford to pay the rent. And while you haven't told me the name of your lover, I imagine you must still be in love with him. So, I would hardly expect you to leap into bed with me,' he'd grinned.

'Quite honestly, Amber, I don't see any reason why two people—who happen to be good friends—shouldn't come together for their mutual benefit. Give yourself time to think about it,' he'd urged before driving her home to her aunt's depressingly gloomy house.

Amber had spent sleepless nights trying to think what to do for the best. But, in the end, it was the desperate need to place a roof over both her mother's and the baby's head that had finally made up her mind. Clive had been delighted at her agreement to marry him, suggesting a quiet register-office wedding in London before their returning to live in Elmbridge.

There had been some gossip, of course, but when Lucy was born, most people seemed pleased that the once hopelessly wild Clive Stanhope had finally settled down and become a sensible, down-to-earth family

man. For her part, Amber had been deeply grateful
to Clive, both for looking after her and the baby, and
his patience with her mother, who'd come to live with
them on leaving hospital. 'I'm very fond of your
mother even if she's sometimes as nutty as a fruit
cake!' he'd laughed. 'In fact, as far as I can see, we've
got years and years of happiness in front of us.'

And so they might have had, if Clive hadn't died
in a car accident when Lucy was barely a year old. It
had been such a deeply unhappy and worrying time
that Amber had barely been able to mourn the loss
of poor Clive. All her energies had been consumed in
the struggle to survive the horrendous financial
problems resulting from his premature death. And
although she'd managed to keep going for the past
seven years, it now seemed dreadfully ironic that Max
should have come back when, for the second time in
her life, she was about to lose the roof over her head.
Surely, if there was any justice in the world, she ought
to be free of the man who'd caused her so much pain
and torment all those years ago?

But as she carried her mother's tray downstairs, she
knew that life was never particularly fair or easy. And
she couldn't help wondering if she'd always known,
deep in her heart, that their brief love affair had been
just a dream within a dream. That the sense of having
found a secret measure of time—with the rest of the
world fading into a grey mist about the sunlit, radiant
figures of Max and herself—had been nothing more
than a foolish delusion.

If so, she'd certainly paid in the past for such folly
in torment and heartache. And now, it seemed, she

was going to have to pay yet again. Because, with Max's return, there seemed absolutely nothing she could do to prevent her whole world from being smashed to smithereens.

Feeling sick and queasy with nervous tension, Amber stared down at the food in front of her, unable to do more than push it around her plate. Unlike Max, who'd demolished a large bowl of soup, together with umpteen slices of fresh brown bread and butter, before finally wolfing down two large helpings of apple pie and cream.

'That was wonderful! As my father, who liked to quote from the Bible, would have said: "A good woman's price is far above rubies",' he grinned, leaning back in his chair as she rose to clear the plates from the table.

'Since your wild, teenage behaviour meant that no housekeeper ever stayed at the vicarage for more than a few weeks, I'm not at all surprised that it was one of your father's favourite quotations,' she retorted sourly. 'Do you want some coffee?'

'Yes, please,' he said before giving a rueful shake of his head. 'You're quite right, of course. Poor old Dad. I really was pretty appalling in those days, wasn't I?'

'Yes, you certainly were.' Tearing her eyes away from his dynamically masculine figure, she tried to control her nervously trembling hands as she scooped freshly ground coffee into a jug before placing the heavy steel kettle on the stove. 'In fact,' she added waspishly, 'I can't see that you've altered in any way.'

He rose slowly to his feet. 'Now, that's where you're quite wrong. Believe me, Amber, it would be a *grave* mistake to think that I'm still the poor, deluded young fool that you once knew,' he drawled, a threatening note of menace underlying his words. 'I can assure you that a great deal of water has passed under the bridge since then.'

'Yes, I'm sure it has,' she muttered before taking a deep breath and forcing herself to turn and face him. 'Look—why don't we cut out all this nonsense and get straight to the point?' she demanded. 'I want to know why it's taken you over three weeks to return here to Elmbridge. And *exactly* what is it you want from me?'

He stared at her in silence for a moment before giving a shrug of his broad shoulders. 'I couldn't return here before now because I've been away in America on business. And we'll come to what I want in a moment. But before doing so—I'd be interested in hearing the answer to a minor question, which has been puzzling me for some time.'

'And that is...?'

'It's ancient history now, of course. But I've often wondered if Clive Stanhope ever found out that you'd been two-timing him with me all those years ago?'

Amber's jaw dropped as she gazed at him in astonishment. Having steeled herself to face yet another interrogation, together with ruthless demands for access to her small daughter, she was now feeling totally bewildered and confused. Two-timing him... with Clive? What on earth was he talking about?

Viewing the girl who was staring at him with dazed, stunned eyes, Max gave another wry shrug of his shoulders. 'It's merely an academic question now, of course, since the guy is dead. But what I've never been able to understand, Amber...' he paused, his lips twisting sardonically as he raised a dark eyebrow, 'is why you were also having an affair with Clive—of all people!'

'You never liked him, did you?'

Max shook his head as her bitter retort seemed to echo around the quiet room. 'No. You're quite right, I didn't,' he agreed slowly. 'I was, of course, genuinely very sorry to hear about his fatal accident. However, to tell the truth, I'd always regarded Clive as basically a spoiled brat—a weak personality with far too much money for his own good. But you clearly thought otherwise, hmm?'

'Yes, I most certainly did! Because, as far as I'm concerned, Clive was one of the nicest men I've ever known,' she retorted furiously. 'He may have gone slightly off the rails when he was younger, and I'd have to admit that he was always fairly hopeless with money. But Clive was basically a sweet, kind-hearted and generous man who was very, *very* good to me,' she added vehemently as Max walked slowly towards her.

He gave a scornful laugh. 'Since you're now living such a comfortable, easy life in one of the largest houses in the district—the sale of which is likely to make you a wealthy woman—it certainly seems that Clive *was* very good to you. Very good indeed!'

'How *dare* you insinuate that I married poor Clive for his money. You... you know absolutely *nothing* about my way of life,' she cried, almost choking with rage and fury.

But when he gave yet another caustic laugh of sheer disbelief, something seemed to snap in Amber's brain. Almost without knowing what she was doing, and intent only on removing that contemptuous, scathing expression from his face, her hand flashed up to slap him hard on the cheek.

There was a long, deathly silence, broken only by the sound of Max's sharp intake of breath as he stared down at her, his blue eyes as hard and cold as ice.

'That was a *very* stupid thing to do,' he grated harshly.

'I... I'm not sorry. It serves you right for being so despicable,' Amber gasped, backing nervously away from his tall, rigidly angry figure, her retreat abruptly halted as she felt her spine jar against the hard steel edge of the sink unit.

'You can't bear to face the truth, can you?' he snarled, raising his hands to clasp hold of her slim shoulders, and staring down into her defiant, angry green eyes. 'And the truth, as we both know, is that you're nothing but a money-grubbing, two-timing bitch!'

'My God, that's rich!' she cried. 'Especially from you, of all people! "First he loved her—then he left her" was *your* theme song, remember?' she ground out bitterly, trying without success to escape from the tall figure looming over her. 'Only, in *my* case, you left me holding the baby. So, if you really want to see a lousy, rotten, two-timing bastard, why not take a good look at yourself in the mirror?'

There was a long silence as the aggression seemed to drain away from Max's stiff, rigid figure, his face pale and strained as he stared intently down at her, his dark brows drawn together in a deep frown.

'Are you seriously trying to tell me . . . ?'

'I wouldn't dream of trying to tell you *anything*. You're the one who claims to know it all,' she snapped nervously as he leaned forward, raising his hands to slowly and deliberately wind his fingers through her golden brown hair.

'I certainly once thought that I knew you,' he murmured.

Amber stiffened, warning bells jangling loudly in her brain as she noted the oddly thick, husky note in his voice. Oh, Heavens! she told herself wildly. She *must* get away from this highly dangerous man—and as quickly as possible.

'Yes, well, we all make mistakes,' she muttered breathlessly, trying to wriggle out from beneath his long, tall figure. But Amber realised that she'd left it too late as she felt his fingers tightening in her hair, holding her firmly imprisoned against him.

Desperately trying to maintain the force of her anger and fury, she was dismayed to find it swiftly draining away. Her senses seemed bemused by the enticing masculine scent of his cologne, while tremors of sensual excitement were rippling through her body in response to the warmth of the long, muscular thighs touching her own.

Despite knowing—who better?—that Max was a cold-hearted Casanova with all the morals of an alley cat, she couldn't seem to control a treacherous weakness from invading her quivering limbs. Time seemed suspended as she felt a hand moving slowly down her back to clasp her tightly about the waist, hot shivers gripping her stomach as he pulled her even closer to his hard, firm body, whose rapidly pounding heart seemed to be beating in unison with her own.

'No!' she gasped, struggling helplessly within the iron strength of his embrace as his dark head came slowly and inexorably down towards her, his mouth possessing her lips in a kiss of such burning intensity that desire seemed to explode like a firework inside her.

Helplessly trying to cling on to reality, she could feel it quickly slipping away in a mist of rising passion. She was only aware of a feverish, long-denied hunger—a compulsive need to respond to the fiercely invasive heat of his tongue, and the erotic touch of the hands sweeping down over her hips, fiercely pulling her soft body even closer to his tall, muscular frame. And it seemed as if she was caught up in a sudden frenzy of desire, moaning helplessly as she raised her arms to clasp him tightly about the neck, convulsively burying her fingers in his dark, curly hair.

'Amber...!' She hardly heard the deep, ragged groan as his lips left hers, feathering down her neck to seek the softly scented hollow at the base of her throat. As he raised a hand to caress the soft curve of her breast, his fingers brushed over the hard firm peak, causing a fierce shaft of pleasure to flash through her trembling figure. Trapped in a dizzy haze of scorching excitement, it was only when she became aware of the increasingly loud, strident whistle from the kettle she'd placed on the stove that cold reality began to break through the thick mist of passion and desire.

'Ignore it!' Max grunted impatiently as she began struggling to release herself from his embrace. But the magic, enchanted spell that he'd woven was now utterly destroyed, and with a sob she tore herself from his arms.

Shaking as if in the grip of a raging fever, her trembling legs almost gave way beneath her as she staggered across the room to the stove. Making sure that she had the safety of the kitchen table between them, she fought to control her ragged breathing, staring at Max in horror and dismay.

What on earth was happening to her? This was the *second* time that she'd found herself in his arms—and in the space of less than two hours. It was almost unbelievable! But unfortunately, and despite his total betrayal of her in the past, it looked as if she was *still* pathetically susceptible to Max's fatal, dark attraction—an attraction that, as she now bitterly reminded herself, had already caused her untold suffering and torment.

'I...I thought you said earlier, upstairs in the bedroom, that you weren't going to make that sort of "mistake", ever again,' she accused him bleakly.

'Yes, I believe I did say something of the sort,' he agreed with a mocking smile.

'So...?' she demanded indignantly.

He gave a careless shrug of his broad shoulders. 'It looks as though I must have changed my mind, doesn't it?'

'Well, you can just change your mind right back again,' she ground out furiously. 'How you had the sheer *nerve* to say all those horrid things...' She waved her hands distractedly in the air. 'I don't care what you say about me, but I won't hear a word against poor Clive.'

'You asked for my opinion of your late husband,' Max pointed out quietly. 'However, I've no wish to speak ill of the dead, and I'm sincerely sorry if I've upset you in any way. After all, it's true to say that I hardly knew the guy, and so...'

'No, you didn't know him at all,' she flashed back indignantly. 'Because, when I was at my lowest ebb—not only having been deserted by you, but desperately worried about my mother, and almost suicidal with panic and fear at finding myself pregnant—it was *Clive Stanhope* who came to my rescue. So, don't you *ever* dare to make any more sneering remarks about a man who, out of the sheer kindness of his heart, provided a home for my family.

'And now,' she continued grimly, pleased to note that Max wasn't attempting to say anything, his face a blank mask as he stared silently at her across the kitchen. 'This seems to be the perfect time to show you over the house. I'm sure that you'll be interested to view my "rich inheritance" and in seeing just what an "easy, comfortable life" I have here,' she added sarcastically, not waiting to see whether he was following her as she stalked angrily from the room.

*   *   *

'Well—have you got the message at last?' she demanded some time later, throwing open the door of yet another room. Like so many of the others that she'd shown him, it was stripped of all carpets, curtains and furniture, consisting only of bare floorboards and blank walls.

Max's increasingly grim, stern expression as he'd followed her silently through the house from one empty room to another should have provided a sweet revenge for all the unkind, malicious remarks that he'd made earlier about her supposedly glamorous lifestyle. But Amber now found herself suddenly feeling weary of the whole exercise.

'There's lots more rooms like this, of course,' she told him with a heavy sigh. 'The truth is that we're more or less flat broke. Clive had gone through most of his inheritance long before he married me. But it didn't seem to matter when he was alive. I was just so happy to have a roof over my head and to be able to look after my mother and the baby. After Clive's death ...' She paused for a moment. 'Well, for the past few years, I've been taking in paying guests to help pay some of the household bills. But now, without going into all the boring details, I'm having to sell this house simply because I can't borrow any more money to feed and clothe the family. In fact,' she gave a wry smile as she waved a tired hand around the empty room, 'your accusation that I married Clive just because he was a rich man now seems to be a bit of a grim joke, doesn't it?'

Max didn't immediately reply, giving her a sharp, penetrating glance from beneath his dark brows before walking slowly across the old oak floorboards covered in dust to gaze blindly out of a window.

'It looks as though I owe you a deep apology,' he said at last, his husky voice echoing eerily in the empty room as he continued to stare through the window at the parkland, now slowly becoming less visible in the softly gathering darkness of the late winter's afternoon. 'It's no excuse, of course, but I just assumed...' He paused, swearing softly under his breath as he brushed a hand roughly through his thick, curly dark hair. 'So, all those old portraits and antique furniture downstairs...?'

'Nothing but pure window dressing,' she told the man, who was still standing with his back to her. 'As you've seen, the entrance hall, sitting and dining rooms are still furnished more or less as they always were. Our own bedrooms are a bit Spartan, with just the basic necessities. However, I've managed to keep three guest-rooms in a fairly decent state, for when we have visitors. But that's it. Everything else went to the saleroom a long time ago.'

'*For God's sake!*' he exploded as he whirled around to face her. 'Why on earth didn't you tell me? I could have taken care of you all. There would have been no need for you to sell either the house or your possessions.' His lips tightened with anger as he gazed about the empty room.

She stared at him, completely dumbfounded for a moment, before leaning weakly against the wall, her slim frame shaking with hysterical laughter. 'Oh, Max, you're absolutely priceless!' She shook her head, lifting a shaking hand to wipe tears of helpless mirth from her eyes.

'I can't see what's so damn funny about your situation!' he grated angrily.

'Because, if I didn't laugh at such a ridiculously stupid statement, I'd probably scream with frustration and rage.' She gave a weary shake of her head. 'For Heaven's sake, I thought you were supposed to be such a clever, successful businessman. Haven't you yet worked out exactly *why* I accepted Clive's kind, generous offer of marriage?'

He shrugged. 'I'd always thought...I just assumed that you'd decided he was a better matrimonial prospect. After all, I hadn't anything to offer you at the time, and...'

'Oh, for goodness' sake, don't be such an idiot,' she retorted impatiently. 'The answer is, in fact, a very simple one. I couldn't tell you *anything* about myself and the baby because I had absolutely no way of contacting you.'

'That's simply not true!' he growled fiercely.

'What isn't true?' she demanded bleakly. 'The fact that you professed undying love and wanted to marry me? Or that after leaving me pregnant, you quickly skipped the country?'

'I promise you, I had absolutely *no* idea that you were expecting a baby,' he assured her earnestly, his face pale beneath its tan as he gazed at her with a tense, strained expression.

'You may not have been aware of my pregnancy— something that even *I* didn't know about until it was far too late. But you'd still disappeared off the face of the earth, making damn sure that I didn't have your new address in America. Right?'

'No! You're damn well *wrong!*' he ground out through clenched teeth, swearing violently under his breath as he began pacing up and down the room. 'How can you possibly believe that I set out to deliberately deceive you? For God's sake, Amber, you must know that I'd never do such a thing.'

'Oh, really?' she enquired with grim irony. 'Well, short of taking up clairvoyance, or placing a "Wanted" poster in every town in the United States, I'll be fascinated to hear just *how* I was supposed to get in touch with you. Even if I'd ever wanted to see you again—which I most certainly did not.'

'You don't understand,' he growled.

'You're quite right,' she snapped. 'I never did "understand" your rotten behaviour. And, quite frankly, it's now far too late for me to care one way or another,' she added with a heavy sigh, suddenly feeling tired to death of the whole wretched story.

So often, in the past, she had dreamed of being able to tell Max exactly what she thought of his vile, treacherous behaviour. But now that he was actually standing here in front of her, it all seemed so pointless somehow. In fact, by raking up the painful events that had taken place so many years ago, it looked as though she'd only succeeded in causing herself even more distress.

'You've got to let me explain . . .'

'Oh, no, I haven't! I'm simply not interested—and it's far too late for any "explanations". It's been eight years since you callously dumped me. Eight years in which I've made a new life for both myself and my daughter. And now, if you'll excuse me...' she added, glancing down at the watch on her wrist, 'I must go and dig up some vegetables before the light goes. Please feel free to continue your tour of this house, which, as we both know, you have no intention of buying,' she added grimly, before swiftly leaving the room.

CHAPTER FIVE

THE clink of glasses and the noisy, cheerful sound of raised voices and laughter filled the large main area of the old Assembly Rooms.

Built in Regency times and carefully preserved by the efforts of the town council, the Assembly Rooms had originally been designed to cater for local meetings, dances and parties—providing a much-needed, central venue for a sparsely populated and rural area. However, as she gazed around the elegant room, filled with so many of her old friends and acquaintances, Amber realised that she and the other local inhabitants of the town were fortunate to still have the use of such a lovely old building.

'The party appears to be going well,' Philip said as he placed a fresh glass of wine in her hand. 'Everyone seems determined to press ahead with strong opposition to the new marina.'

'But it's going to be difficult to save the Tide Mill,' she sighed. 'Especially since the developers have already been given planning permission to pull it down.'

'Well, with snow forecast for the weekend, I don't reckon there will be much building work taking place—not until the new year, at least,' he pointed out. 'I just wish that I could say the same for my own profession. Unfortunately, this is by far my busiest time of the year.'

Amber looked at him with concern. 'I know you've been very busy this week. Are you on call again tonight?'

'I'm afraid so.' The young doctor gave her a tired grin. 'However, let's hope that all my patients stay well and healthy—for the duration of this party, at least! Incidentally, have I told you about the plans for my new surgery? I'm really very excited about the layout, and...'

But as Philip continued to expand on his architect's ideas for the new building, Amber suddenly stiffened, her green eyes widening in shock as the crowd of people parted for a moment, and she caught a glimpse of the tall, dark figure of a man standing across the room.

Max...? What on earth was he doing here? she asked herself, suddenly feeling panic-stricken as she watched his hard, determined features relaxing into a courteous smile as he turned to shake someone's hand.

How could she have been so stupid? She might have known that it was useless to try and avoid his baleful presence. But when she'd taken refuge in the kitchen garden—leaving Max to continue looking over a house which she was certain he had no intention of buying— she still hadn't been entirely convinced that he was seriously intending to stay at Elmbridge Hall. He had, after all, only returned to the town in order to see Lucy. And once he'd discovered that she wasn't due to return until tomorrow, surely Max would prefer the more convivial, lively atmosphere to be found in one of the small local hotels.

A bout of hard digging in the kitchen garden had, as always, helped to soothe her battered spirits. Although she'd eventually been driven back inside by a light snowfall and the gathering darkness, Amber had felt able to view the day's sequence of events in a slightly calmer frame of mind than when she'd first stormed out of the house.

It was, of course, no good trying to fudge the issue: she'd been a perfect idiot. Not only had she been guilty of underestimating Max's sheer ruthlessness, but also totally stupid to have allowed herself to be alone with him. Why hadn't she remembered that a leopard never changes his spots? That even as a teenager, he'd been like the awful nursery-rhyme character, Georgie-Porgie, 'who kissed the girls and made them cry'? Just about a *perfect* description of Max Warner—the root cause of so many tears and so much unhappiness in her life. But never, *never* again, Amber had grimly promised herself, returning to the house full of good intentions and firm resolve.

Pleased to discover that both Max and his car had disappeared, she knew that she hadn't seen the last of him—especially as he had yet to state his intentions regarding Lucy. However, when he still hadn't returned by the time she'd prepared an early supper for her mother, and Philip Jackson had arrived to give her a lift to the party, Amber had allowed herself to hope that he might even have decided to go back to London.

Fat chance! she told herself, staring glumly down at her glass. Goodness knows, she hadn't really wanted to come here tonight. But it had seemed important, if only for Lucy's sake, to try and appear to be behaving as normally as possible.

Attempting to pull herself together and concentrate on Philip's remarks about the plans for his new surgery, she heard the pager, which the doctor always carried in the top pocket of his jacket, give a sharp, high-pitched 'bleep'.

'I thought it was too good to last,' he told her ruefully, bending down to give her a quick peck on the cheek before hurrying off across the room in search of a telephone.

Sipping her wine and hoping that Philip wouldn't be long, Amber was startled when a hard, familiar voice spoke from behind her shoulder.

'Has the good doctor left you all alone? What a shame.'

Spinning around, she glared up at Max, who was grinning wolfishly down at her.

'He happens to be on call tonight,' she snapped before realising that Max must have been doing his homework. How else would he have known that Philip was a doctor? 'What are you doing here?' she demanded. 'I can't believe you're interested in what happens to the old Tide Mill?'

'Oh, I'm interested in all sorts of things,' he drawled. 'For instance, I'm looking forward to seeing how much the town has changed, meeting old friends and acquaintances, seeing Lucy...'

'I'm not prepared to talk about my daughter—certainly not *here*!' she retorted, glancing nervously around to see if anyone else had heard what he was saying.

'*Our* daughter,' he corrected smoothly.

'OK...OK!' she muttered, feeling almost sick with tension. Didn't Max know or care about the torture he was putting her through?

'You're quite right. This is neither the time nor the place for that sort of discussion,' he murmured, pausing for a moment as a waiter topped up their glasses. 'So...maybe we could discuss our own relationship instead?'

'What "relationship"?' she ground out through clenched teeth. 'As far as I'm concerned, we have absolutely nothing in common—except a very brief, unfortunate episode in the past. So, why don't you leave me alone? Go off and play your rotten games with someone else. And there's *just* the perfect companion for you,' she added grimly, nodding her head towards a noisy group of men, surrounding a beautifully dressed, glamorous ash-blonde woman. 'I hear that your old flame, Cynthia Henderson, can't wait to meet you again. And since everyone knows that Cynthia can never resist a man with a large bank balance, I'm sure she'll welcome *you* with open arms!' Amber taunted, not caring if she was sounding like a first-class bitch in her determination to hit back at him.

'Well, it certainly looks as if it's my lucky day, doesn't it?' he drawled sardonically. 'Because I thought that *your* arms seemed remarkably welcoming this afternoon.'

'Oh, shut up!' she snapped, her cheeks flushing with embarrassment and the realisation that she could never seem to get the better of this indomitable man.

Luckily, she was rescued from having to say anything more by the approach of Sally's husband, John Fraser.

'Hello, Amber, you're looking as lovely as ever,' the lawyer smiled at her. 'I'm sorry to be a nuisance, but I wonder if I could just have a quick word with Max? There are one or two people who would like to meet him, and...'

'Sure,' Max agreed quickly, promising to return in a moment, before following the lawyer back across the room.

Fervently hoping that she'd seen the last of Max, at least for this evening, Amber realised that she had a problem. However much she might want to leave this party as soon as possible, she had no way of getting home. With her old Land Rover in the local garage, and Philip busy with his sick patients, she was well and truly stuck. Desperately trying to find a solution to her dilemma, she was surprised to see Cynthia Henderson gliding purposefully across the floor towards her.

By far the most grown-up and attractive girl at school, Cynthia had managed to avoid the dire fate that—according to her teachers and the mothers of the other pupils in the class—lay in wait for such a boy-mad, sexually promiscuous teenager. Cynthia had, in fact, matured into a very glamorous and distractingly beautiful woman. Marrying and discarding at least two husbands along the way, she was now the owner of a very expensive boutique in the centre of town.

'Been abandoned, have you?' Cynthia drawled as she came nearer. 'Men really are the pits, aren't they?' she added, lighting a cigarette and casually blowing smoke in the other girl's face.

'You may have a point there,' Amber agreed grimly, raising a hand to fan the fumes from her eyes.

'Of course I do, sweetie,' Cynthia murmured, her eyes flicking contemptuously over Amber's plain black dress, which had clearly seen better days. 'I mean— just look at those stupid women.' She waved an el- egant, crimson-nailed hand around the room. 'As soon as they set eyes on darling Max, they all im- mediately went on "red alert". A total waste of time, of course. You couldn't expect such an attractive man to even give them the time of day!' she added with a cruel laugh. 'By the way, I hear Max is staying at your boarding-house for a few days.'

'Yes,' Amber told her stonily, not finding it at all difficult to understand why Cynthia was so deeply unpopular with the other women in the town.

'Well, I don't suppose he'll be with you for long. As far as I can see, it looks as if Max hasn't changed one bit.' She gave another low, throaty chuckle of laughter. 'Because, if I remember rightly—and of course I do!—he always did get bored *very* easily.'

Amber shrugged, steeling herself against the poisonous darts of this equally poisonous woman, who was clearly intent on reclaiming her old boyfriend.

Well, the very best of luck to her! Amber thought sourly. If Max wanted to get heavily involved with this sexy, ash-blonde divorcee, that was entirely his own affair. She didn't give a toss *what* he did—just as long as he left her and Lucy alone. Right?

Unexpectedly overwhelmed by a sudden heavy weight of depression, her dismal thoughts were sharply interrupted as Cynthia gave a quick, breathless gasp of pleasure.

'Max, darling! How *wonderful* to see you again!' she cried as his tall, rangy figure crossed the room towards them. 'It was very naughty of you to abandon poor little Amber....' she added, winding her arms about his neck and giving him a long, lingering kiss on the lips.

Try as she might, Amber couldn't seem able to tear her eyes away from the glamorous blonde's voluptuous figure pressed so closely to that of Max, or to avoid noticing the way in which he was so enthusiastically responding to her kiss, his hands eagerly closing about her slim waist.

'Umm...we must *definitely* do that again—very soon!' Cynthia gave another husky, sensual laugh as she slowly removed her arms from around his neck. 'The whole town is buzzing with news of the prodigal's return. Is it *really* true that you're thinking of settling down here in Elmbridge?' she added, gazing hungrily up into his gleaming blue eyes.

Amber froze, her nails biting into the palms of her tightly clenched hands as she realised that the feelings tearing at her heart with such sharp, fierce claws were nothing more or less than an overwhelming surge of pure feminine jealousy. Feeling faint and almost sick, she stared down at the floor while she struggled to control her emotions. Like an animal in pain, she wanted only to escape, to seek the shelter of a deep, dark and private burrow in which to lick her wounds in secret. But of course, she couldn't. Sunk in misery, it was some time before she became fully aware of the conversation taking place beside her.

'...yes, I'll be in touch with you again, very soon. Unfortunately, I'm afraid that it's time Amber and I were on our way.'

'What...?'

'I've just bumped into your boyfriend,' he told Amber, who was staring at him in glassy-eyed horror. 'He was just rushing off to a bad car accident on the A45. Apparently it looks as if we're in for a heavy snowstorm tonight. So I said that I'd take you back home.'

'Surely there's no need to leave so soon?' Cynthia murmured, obviously not at all pleased by the turn of events. 'I'm dying to hear what you've been doing all these years you've been away. And is it really true that you're thinking of settling down here in Elmbridge? It would be such fun helping you to find just the *right* house. There are quite a few on the market at the moment, and...'

'Oh, that's no problem. I've already decided to buy Elmbridge Hall.'

'What a brilliant idea!' she exclaimed happily over Amber's muffled gasp of protest. 'And once you've renovated that poor, neglected house, there's only one more thing you'll need to make everything just *perfect*.'

'And that is?'

'Surely it's obvious darling. What you need is a wife!' Cynthia murmured huskily, throwing him a smouldering, sideways glance through her long, thick eyelashes.

'You're absolutely right,' Max agreed. 'In fact, I'm hoping to get married to an old girlfriend in the very near future.'

And we all know which 'old girlfriend' he has in mind, Amber thought miserably as Max led her from the room. If that smile of smug satisfaction and triumph on the glamorous divorcee's face was any-thing to go by, the only question in Cynthia's mind was precisely where she and Max would be spending their honeymoon.

The heavy, oppressive silence within Max's car seemed never-ending. As did the short journey back to Elmbridge Hall. Tense and nervous, Amber stared blindly through the windscreen, the rapidly falling snow glistening in the bright glare of the headlights. She could hardly believe that it was still only Friday night. Just how long was she going to have to put up with the ominous, baleful presence of this hard and indomitable man?

Desperately trying to combat a rising tide of fear and panic, Amber closed her eyes and leaned back against the headrest. It was nerve-racking to realise that they *still* hadn't discussed the all-important matter of Lucy. Or could it be that Max was just playing a

game with her? Maybe he was deliberately keeping
her in this ghastly state of overwhelming stress and
anxiety, piling on the agony until almost the last
moment before his departure.

And that wasn't all. On top of all her other
problems, she now had to contend with his apparent
decision to buy Elmbridge Hall. How *dare* he just
casually announce the news to that nauseating woman,
Cynthia Henderson? Surely he might have had the
common decency to discuss the matter with her before
telling anyone else. After all, it *was* still her home. It
was up to *her* to decide whether or not she wished to
sell it to Max.

Amber could almost tangibly feel the anger and fury
raging through her veins at being treated as though
she had no choice in the matter. For all he knew, there
might be hundreds of people queuing up to purchase
the Hall. The unfortunate fact that Max was the only
person who'd expressed any interest in purchasing the
old Tudor mansion merely served to increase her frustration at being treated in such a high-handed manner.

By the time Max brought the car to a halt outside
Elmbridge Hall, she'd worked herself up into such a
state that she could contain herself no longer. 'What
are you intending to do about Lucy?' she burst out
angrily as he came around to open her door. 'And if
you think you can just calmly announce that you're
going to buy my home, you've got another think
coming!'

'I suggest we leave any discussion on those points
until we get inside. It's freezing out here,' Max said,
taking hold of her arm and leading her trembling

figure up the icy steps to the front door. 'Why don't you go and check that your mother's all right?' he added as they entered the house.

'Why don't you mind your own damn business—and stop ordering me around?' she retorted furiously before stalking off across the hall towards Violet Grant's wing of the house.

After checking on her mother, who was fast asleep, Amber was still fuming by the time she made her way to the sitting room, where Max had set out a tray containing a bottle and two glasses. Casting a jaundiced eye over the large flagon of rare malt whiskey—it was years since she'd been able to afford anything so expensive—she was slightly mollified by the fact that Max had also put some more logs on the smouldering fire in the huge grate, whose flames cast a warm glow over the antique furniture and old velvet curtains.

'Here . . . this will warm you up,' he said, holding out a glass of pale tawny liquid towards her.

Backing away from him, she shook her head. 'No, I don't want anything more to drink. I've already had a lot of wine at dinner, and . . .'

'For God's sake, relax!' he retorted impatiently, firmly placing the glass in her hands. 'Believe me, this is purely medicinal. Far from intending to seduce you with the demon drink, I'm merely trying to prevent you from looking quite so cold and tired.'

'I really don't . . .'

'Drink it!' he growled, frowning fiercely down at her until she did as she was told before leading her towards a comfortable sofa by the fire.

'Whatever happened to the glamorous and charming "Mad Max" Warner? From what I can see, you appear to have all the charisma of a rattlesnake!' she grumbled, determined not to admit that the fiery liquor was indeed making her feel a good deal warmer —and less weary.

'I've already told you to forget the past,' he told her firmly, sitting himself down on the other end of the sofa. 'I'm only interested in the present—and the future, of course. Which is why I want to discuss what we're going to do about Lucy.'

Overwhelmingly relieved to find that Max was, at last, prepared to broach the subject that had been tormenting her for so many weeks, Amber took a deep breath. Whatever the provocation, it was desperately important that she remain cool, calm and collected throughout their discussion.

'I know Elmbridge has changed and grown slightly larger since you've been away. But it is still a small market town, with everyone taking a close friendly interest in their neighbours. In other words,' she gave him a weak smile, 'it's very much the same hotbed of rumour and gossip that it's always been.'

He shrugged. 'You're not telling me anything that I haven't already seen and heard for myself.'

'Well, bully for you!' she exclaimed impatiently. 'However, I've lived in Elmbridge all my life, and Lucy was born and raised here. So, you can take it from me, that it's only going to need *one* person to see the both of you together, and just about everyone else will know—inside twenty-four hours—that Clive had to marry me because I was expecting your illegitimate baby. But that's only one small part of the problem,' she added quickly as he stirred restlessly on the sofa. 'You obviously don't give a hoot about *my* good name—but what about Lucy? She's only a little girl and hardly knows you from Adam. Can't you imagine the shock and distress she's going to feel, suddenly confronted by the fact that Clive wasn't really her father? Not to mention the poor child having to put up with being teased and laughed at by all her schoolfriends. I won't have her being subjected to...to that sort of ordeal!' Amber glared at him, her fists clenched tightly in her lap. 'There's *no way* that I'll let you ruin her life!'

'For goodness' sake, calm down!' he told her sternly. 'I'm well aware of the problems we have to face.'

'There won't be any "problems"—not if you drop your daft idea of buying this house,' she retorted quickly. 'All you have to do is to go straight back to London, or whatever, and I'll make sure that Lucy visits you as often as you like. We can take our time in explaining that you're her real father, and that way there won't be any need for...'

'No.' He gave a firm shake of his dark head. 'No, I'm afraid that idea of yours won't work.'

'But why not? So, OK, you've inherited your grandmother's estate. But that doesn't necessarily mean you *have* to live in Elmbridge,' she pointed out, striving to sound calm and reasonable. 'Even if you're fed up with London, there's bound to be some marvellous houses for sale not too far away. What about Cambridge, for instance? It's a lovely university town,

full of interesting people and only an hour away by
car from Elmbridge. On top of which, there's the Arts
Theatre, regular concerts in the Guildhall, and——'
She broke off as she saw his lips twitching with sup-
pressed laughter. 'I don't see what's so damn funny,'
she ground out through clenched teeth, desperately
striving to control an overwhelming urge to slap that
supercilious grin off his face.

'I was merely amused by your sales pitch for the
City of Cambridge,' he drawled. 'However, while I
agree that it's a lovely town, I can assure you that I
am definitely returning to live in Elmbridge, and that
I have every intention of buying this house.'

'But... but I don't see *why* ...' Amber wailed, suddenly forced to realise that she had no hope of getting
this arrogant man to listen to any sound, logical arguments. 'Haven't you *any* idea of what you'll be
doing to my family? Surely you ought to be able to
understand...' She waved a hand helplessly in the air.

'I've heard a great deal regarding how *you* feel
about the situation,' he retorted grimly. 'How about
trying to understand *my* feelings for a change?'

'What... what are you talking about?'

'Have you actually bothered to think about anyone
other than yourself? To wonder how *I* must have felt
on suddenly discovering that I had a daughter?' he
demanded scathingly before rising impatiently to his
feet and striding about the room. 'Well, since it obviously hasn't, I can tell you that I was completely
and utterly shattered! One moment I was merely
calling to view a house, which I'd been told was for
sale, and then...' He brushed a distracted hand

through his thick, curly dark hair. 'For God's sake, Amber, that child is the spitting image of me. How in the hell did you think you could get away with claiming that Clive Stanhope was Lucy's father?'

'Clive had dark hair, although his was straight, of course. But children often have curly hair when they're young...' she muttered, her cheeks reddening as he gave a caustic snort of derision. 'Besides, you'd left the area years ago. There was no reason for anyone to make the connection between you and Lucy.'

'Did you ever intend to tell her the truth?'

'No, why should I?' Amber retorted defiantly. 'You'd had your fun before callously deserting me and my unborn child. I didn't—and I still don't, for that matter—see any reason for upsetting Lucy or causing her any distress by telling her that Clive wasn't her father. In fact, there was absolutely no problem. Not until you suddenly appeared out of nowhere— like the demon king in a pantomime,' she added bitterly.

'Thanks!'

'Well, what do you expect? I'm hardly likely to hang out the flags and cry "whoopee!" Not like your old girlfriend, Cynthia.' She gave a shrill, high-pitched laugh. '*You* may have only been back in the town for a day, but it looks as though *she's* already chosen her wedding dress, and all set for a quick canter up the aisle!'

'Can we please keep to the point at issue,' Max told her brusquely. Although he did not, she noted grimly, disagree with her assessment: that Cynthia was hell-bent on marrying him as soon as possible. 'My only concern at the moment is how both you and I can come to a sensible decision regarding Lucy's future. That's what you want, isn't it?' he demanded, sitting down on the sofa beside her.

'What I want... what I want is for you to go away and leave us alone!'

'Well, I'm afraid that isn't going to happen. Come on, Amber, you must try and pull yourself together,' he said in a softer tone of voice, taking her trembling hands in his. 'You may wish me a million miles away. But unfortunately, there are several good and valid reasons—inheriting my grandmother's estate, for instance—why I need to live in this area. I could possibly remain based in London, of course. But since I'm going to be visiting Elmbridge on a regular basis, you must see that it wouldn't be long before people started talking about the startling resemblance between Lucy and myself.

'I realise that my business trip to America came at a very bad time,' he continued as she remained silent, her cheeks flushed as she stared down at her fingers clasped within his large hands. 'However, once I'd recovered from the initial shock of discovering that I had a daughter, it did give me three weeks in which to think matters out. To decide on the best course of action—as far as Lucy is concerned. You and I may have messed up our lives,' he added sternly, 'but I'm sure you'll agree that we must try and do better for our child.'

She nodded, unable to speak because of a sudden heavy lump in her throat.

'First and foremost, I want to see as much of Lucy as I can,' he said firmly. 'It may not have been anyone's fault. But the fact remains that I've been denied any knowledge of her existence for the past seven years. I have no intention of being shut out of her life any longer.'

'But... but it will be such a shock. I... I haven't told her anything about the situation,' Amber protested tearfully.

'Relax! There's absolutely no need for you to get into such a state,' he said, placing a large white handkerchief in her trembling fingers. 'I'm perfectly capable of realising that we'll need time to get to know one another. Just as you must realise that I have no intention of trying to interfere with her place in your life. Or her memories of Clive.'

'Lucy was only a baby when he died,' Amber muttered, dabbing her eyes. 'But I have tried to tell her as much as I can about him, so she didn't feel too different from her friends.'

'You've obviously done a splendid job rearing our daughter. From what little I've seen, she appears to be a delightful child,' he told her warmly.

'Yes... yes, she really is,' Amber assured him, nervously twisting the handkerchief in her fingers. 'But, even if you do want to get to know Lucy, I can't see how to manage it. I mean... I know it's totally pathetic to care what people might say or do when the news leaks out. But how can I possibly explain what happened all those years ago? Absolutely *everyone* thinks that Clive is Lucy's father. I know you didn't like him,' she added, weak tears of tiredness filling her eyes and spilling out down over her cheeks. 'But I owe him more than I can say. Without his help and support I'd have been completely destitute, with no choice but to have the baby adopted. Do please try to understand,' she begged. 'I really can't *bear* the thought of Clive being made to look foolish in any way.'

'There's no need to cry,' Max murmured softly, taking the handkerchief from her shaking hands and carefully wiping the tears from her eyes. 'I now realise that I was completely wrong about Clive, and I'm really very grateful that he was able to come to your aid. You have my word that I'll never do anything that is likely to harm his memory.'

Amber leaned back against the cushions with a heavy sigh. 'I still can't see any answer to the problem.'

'Well, I've given the matter a considerable amount of thought, and as far as I can see, there appears to be only one sensible course of action. First of all, I intend to phone Mr Glover tomorrow morning, confirming that I have definitely decided to buy this house. As you've already pointed out, Elmbridge hasn't changed much while I've been away.' He gave her a sardonic grin. 'So, I imagine it will only take twenty-four hours for everyone to know about the sale...?'

Amber gave a weary nod. 'That's probably a conservative estimate,' she agreed listlessly.

'Right. So the scenario for public consumption is going to be a very simple one. Returning home after spending some years abroad—and anxious to settle down at last—I approached Mr Glover, who brought me here to view the house. Whereupon I promptly fell in love with this huge old Tudor mansion... *and* with its owner. So, the poor young widow— bravely struggling to support her aged mother and small daughter—agrees to marry the wealthy prince and they both live happily ever after. It is, as I'm sure you'll agree, a deeply romantic story,' he pointed out, his broad shoulders shaking with amusement. 'And one guaranteed to bring a tear to the eye of even the most hardened cynic.'

It was some moments before Amber, bone-weary and exhausted, was fully able to comprehend what he was saying.

'You must be crazy!' she gasped, sitting bolt upright and staring with horror up into his handsome face.

'On the contrary—it all makes perfect sense,' he drawled with a sardonic grin, completely ignoring her strangled protests of rage and fury as he continued to outline his proposed scenario.

'Since I've spent so many years in the United States—where life is, of course, lived at a much faster pace—everyone will quite understand my reluctance to hang around, once I'd made up my mind to a course of action. And what could be nicer than a Christmas wedding? Nothing flashy, of course, just a small, simple affair. And then, while this house is being put in order, we'll fly off to Switzerland for a combined honeymoon and skiing holiday. Which will give me a perfect opportunity to get to know Lucy.'

'I...I've never heard such stuff and nonsense!'

'It's the only possible solution to the problem,' he retorted firmly. 'My daughter needs a father. And I'm *quite* determined that she's going to have one.'

'So, OK, I may well get married to someone in the future. But not to you, of all people!' Amber cried, almost beside herself with rage. Who in the hell did this awful man think he was? God's gift to women?

Max gave a bark of caustic laughter. 'I hope you're not thinking of involving that young doctor in your plans. He's quite the wrong man for you.'

'What...what right have you to interfere in my friendship with Philip?' she gasped.

'As Lucy's father, I've obviously got strong views on the subject,' he drawled smoothly. 'Believe me, there's no way I'd approve of Philip Jackson.'

'What damned cheek!' Amber ground out, almost choking with fury. 'Well, I don't give *that* for your so-called "approval".' She snapped her fingers in his face. 'It's about time you realised that you have absolutely no rights as far as Lucy is concerned. And, in any case, you obviously know nothing about Philip,' she added defiantly. 'Because he's a very sweet, caring man, who's going to make someone a wonderful husband.'

'You may be right. But that's pure speculation because you're certainly not marrying him. As for my "rights" regarding Lucy...' His eyes hardened into frosty chips of blue ice. 'It would be *very* foolish of you to even think of denying me access.'

'I'm not listening to any more...I won't be threatened like this!' Amber lashed back angrily. She jumped to her feet, but her attempt to escape was foiled as he quickly reached up to clasp hold of her hands, pulling her back down on the sofa towards him. 'Let me go!' she panted, struggling helplessly against the iron grip of the fingers tightening cruelly about her wrists.

'It's not a threat—it's a *fact*,' he grated harshly. 'A quick blood test will instantly prove that I'm Lucy's father. And since I'm now a very rich man, I can easily afford to keep you tied up in the courts—until Doomsday, if necessary. Do you *really* want to spend the next few years harassed by a never-ending series of legal writs and injunctions? To have all the gory details of Lucy's conception and birth widely reported in the newspapers? It certainly won't do much for your mother's quality of life, will it?' he continued relentlessly, not bothering to hide the cruel, implacable menace in his voice. 'And what about our daughter? How do you think Lucy will feel as she grows older and realises that she's been deliberately prevented from seeing her real father? I'm told that young teenagers can be very difficult to handle. Quite frankly, Amber, I don't think that she'll ever forgive you.'

'You . . . you *devil*!' Amber gasped in horror, the blood draining from her face.

He shook his head. 'I'm merely trying to get you to see sense. To realise that I'm in deadly earnest.'

'This idea of a marriage is totally . . . utterly impossible! It would never work. That stupid story of yours . . . it's full of holes a mile wide,' she gabbled hysterically. 'No one...absolutely *no one* could possibly believe such a load of old rubbish. Not for one moment!'

'Oh, yes they will,' he retorted confidently. 'Everyone loves a romantic story, especially one that ends with the two lovers going off into the sunset together, hand in hand. In fact, now I think about it,' he mused reflectively, 'we might embellish the tale by letting it become known that I was crazy about you before I went to America. Only you, of course, were far too young. So, I've had to wait all these years before being able to claim my own true love. What do you think?'

'What do I think...?' Amber shrieked, her body shaking with baffled rage and fury as she tried to wriggle free of his grip. 'I think you must be completely *insane*. "A romantic story"? "My own true love"? Who do you think you're kidding?' she grated savagely. 'We both know that you were *never* in love with me. All you were interested in was sex!'

'And you...?' He raised a dark, sardonic eyebrow. 'Were you ever really in love with me?'

'Yes, of course I was,' she snapped, bitterly aware of a deep, hot flush rapidly spreading over her cheeks as she found herself being pulled closer to his broad torso. 'But only because I was far too young and stupid to know any better. Eight years on—it's now a *very* different story. I feel nothing for you. Absolutely nothing at all.'

He gave a low, husky laugh. 'Maybe we ought to test that last statement of yours,' he mocked softly, letting go of her hands, his strong arms closing firmly about her trembling body. 'Because I think you're still crazy about me.'

'You...you arrogant swine! Haven't you heard a word I've been saying?' she demanded breathlessly, desperately trying to free herself from the embrace of the man whose face was now only inches away from her own.

'I don't think you're telling me the truth,' he murmured, studying her intently as his arms tightened about her like bands of steel.

'Oh, yes—yes, I *am*!' she protested, frantically trying to tear her gaze away from the gleam in his glittering blue eyes and the cruel, sensual line of his lips, the message they conveyed suddenly causing her stomach to churn wildly with shock and sexual tension. Staring up mesmerised as the black head came slowly down towards her, she couldn't seem to stop herself from shaking and quivering in response to the sudden fierce, deep hunger flooding through her body as he lowered her back against the cushions, almost holding her breath until his mouth firmly possessed her tremulous lips.

A second later she found herself swept up in a whirlwind of confused sensations. She was intensely aware of the fragrant aroma of his cologne and the warm, firm texture of his skin. Frantically striving to hang on to reality, she seemed unable to prevent her own senses from betraying her. Once again, the barriers which she'd so carefully erected against this man were being destroyed by the sweet seduction of his lips. With a faint, helpless moan she surrendered to the fierce wild excitement of his deepening kiss, the overwhelming need and desire for the caressing touch of his hands on her soft, trembling body.

It seemed a long time before Max raised his dark head to stare intently down at the figure in his arms. 'You may be a very desirable woman, Amber,' he whispered huskily, slowly running a finger down over her flushed cheek. 'But you always were a rotten liar!'

She gazed up at him in bewilderment and confusion, still dazed by the sudden assault on her newly awakened senses. As the heat and desire of a few moments before began slowly ebbing away from her trembling body, her vision was filled by the hard, ruthless gleam in his eyes, the sardonic curve of his lips betraying both mockery and satisfaction. A deep tide of crimson swept over her face and she almost groaned out loud, appalled at the pathetically spineless, feeble way in which—once again—she'd so weakly succumbed to his dark attraction.

Swiftly wriggling free of his relaxed grip, Amber quickly jumped up from the sofa.

'Just a minute,' Max drawled coolly, putting out a hand to catch hold of her wrist as she turned to flee from the room. 'I'm still waiting to hear your decision about our marriage.'

'What marriage?' she bit out savagely through nervous, chattering teeth as she jerked herself free. 'I wouldn't marry *you*—not even if you were the last man on earth!'

'Oh, yes, I'm very sure you will,' Max drawled flatly as she bolted across the room towards the door, his bark of harsh, sardonic laughter echoing in her ears as she stumbled up the stairs to the refuge of her bedroom.

CHAPTER SIX

A SHRILL ringing from the clock beside her bed broke through Amber's restless sleep. Yawning, she put out a hand to silence the alarm before raising her weary head to check the time. Eight o'clock—and time to get up.

Amber groaned, turning over to bury her face in the pillows. Tossing and turning throughout the night, she'd hardly had a wink of sleep. And it was all Max Warner's fault. Lying wide awake through the long hours of darkness, she'd been finally forced to accept that he was quite right. She really *was* still crazy about him! Even thinking about that torrid embrace last night was enough to set her stomach churning wildly, like a cement-mixer out of control. How on earth was she going to stagger through what promised to be a hideously long day?

If *only* she had some experience to fall back on. Some knowledge of both men and the world outside the provincial backwater in which she'd lived for most of her twenty-six years. Unfortunately, having fallen madly in love with Max at the age of eighteen, her subsequent pregnancy and marriage to Clive Stanhope had prevented her from taking part in the normal life of most teenagers. While her contemporaries had been going through the natural process of growing up— gaining some experience of the world and their own sexuality—she'd been looking after a small baby and, before the year was out, mourning the death of her young husband.

It was cringingly embarrassing to realise that her friends would undoubtedly react with screams of laughter, ridicule and sheer disbelief if they ever learned the truth. How could she possibly confess, even to Rose Thomas, that Max had been her first and only lover? That she now felt badly frightened, and completely out of her depth in trying to deal with such a hard, tough and sophisticated man?

With a heavy sigh of deep depression, Amber threw back the covers and swung her feet off the bed. Sitting on the edge of the mattress and staring blindly down at the floor, she realised that she had to pull herself together. Having to face the disastrous truth that she was still in love with Max was only a minor problem compared to the all-important fact that Lucy would be coming home later on this morning. She *must* try to work out exactly how she was going to handle the situation. Max was obviously a whiz at business affairs, but he clearly wasn't used to dealing with a seven-year-old little girl. And while she didn't really believe he would demand that Lucy should immediately be told he was her real father, he was plainly determined to push ahead with his mad idea concerning their marriage. He'd also made it clear that if she didn't agree to his plans for a Christmas wedding, he wouldn't hesitate to carry out his vile, cruel threats to keep her tied up in the courts for ever and a day, destroying both the life of herself and her daughter. So far, none of her protests or arguments had appeared to make the slightest bit of difference. What could she say, or do, that would make him change his mind?

Drawing back the curtains of her bedroom, she saw that there had been a heavy fall of snow during the night. The garden was now covered by a thick white blanket. Glancing up at the heavy grey sky overhead, Amber had no doubt that although it may have stopped snowing for the moment, it wouldn't be long before it started again.

By the time she was downstairs in the kitchen, preparing the breakfast trays for her mother and their guest, she was still feeling deeply depressed at having made no progress in finding an answer to her many problems. In what was clearly an either-or situation, Max seemed to hold all the cards. And it wasn't just the fact that he was insisting that she marry him. What about Lucy? What sort of father would he make for her little girl? Goodness knows it wasn't easy to be a parent these days. It was so important to try and set your children a good example, to bring them up in a steady, responsible manner, which you hoped would give them a sound foundation for their future life. But words like 'steady' and 'responsible' certainly weren't those she associated with Max's past behaviour. Was he likely to change his ways? Was he—hell! she thought grimly, recalling the disgusting way he'd so enthusiastically kissed Cynthia. And the glamorous divorcee had also made it blatantly obvious that, given half a chance, she'd happily jump into his bed.

How could she bear to marry a man who'd not only cruelly deserted her, but who had obviously spent most of his adult life having affairs with one beautiful woman after another? Let's hope he hadn't left any of *them* holding a baby, she told herself bitterly as she placed fresh, warm croissants and toast on his breakfast tray.

Not for the first time, Amber dearly wished that she'd never had the idea of taking in paying guests, which had enabled Max to gain a foothold in the house—something he'd never have been able to do in a private house. Praying that her visitor had passed a thoroughly uncomfortable night, she stomped aggressively up the stairs, not bothering to knock as she threw open the guest-room door, quite happy to chuck his tray at the awful man if he so much as dared to say a word out of place.

Unfortunately, far from still being fast asleep, Max had obviously been up for some time, having already shaved and had a shower. Amber gave him a quick, apprehensive glance, her cheeks flaming with embarrassment as she realised that the tall figure standing across the room was clearly naked, save for a short white towel about his slim hips.

'You must be a mind-reader,' he smiled. 'I was wondering about the arrangements for breakfast.'

'Yes...um...our guests normally prefer to eat breakfast in their rooms,' she muttered breathlessly, trying to tear her eyes away from the sight of his fit, lithe body. The faint drops of moisture still glistened on the bronze skin of his broad shoulders and the hard, muscular chest liberally covered with thick black hair.

Her heart seemed to be pounding like a sledge-hammer, her pulse racing out of control as she desperately wished that she'd stayed down in the kitchen, well away from the sight of his strong, powerful frame and the long, tanned brown legs beneath that ridiculously small towel.

His eyes gleamed with unconcealed mockery as he walked slowly towards her. 'Poor Amber, you look tired. Didn't you sleep very well?' he drawled, his mouth curving with amusement.

'No, I didn't!' she snapped, backing nervously towards the door.

'Relax—there's no need to act like a frightened virgin,' he grinned. 'It's not as though we haven't seen each other's naked bodies in the past.'

'It's not an experience I'm in any hurry to repeat!' she retorted grimly, quickly placing the tray down on a nearby table, the infuriating sound of his laughter echoing behind her as she made a speedy exit from the room.

For the next hour or so, it seemed as though she was in a complete daze. She realised that she must have collected her mother's tray (wild horses wouldn't have dragged her back upstairs to Max's room again), done the washing up and run a vacuum over the carpets in the downstairs rooms. But she had no recollection of having done so. She couldn't seem to think of anything but Lucy's imminent return, and the catastrophic result of Max's strong, sensual appeal on her fragile emotions.

Goodness knows, she had tried to guard and protect herself, rightly fearing the impact of his overpowering attraction on her heart. But it was now far too late for any such dire warnings. In the past, she'd always regarded her love for Max as some sort of sickness or virus, from which she had slowly recovered over the years. How could she have guessed that it was a terminal illness—an acute infection that had no cure? How, when he'd treated her so badly, could she *still* be so deeply in love with him?

Her distressing, gloomy thoughts were interrupted by a phone call from the local garage, informing her that her old Land Rover was ready for collection. Gratefully thanking the mechanic for having fixed it so quickly, she was surprised by the man's chuckle of amusement.

'I wish all my jobs were that easy,' he told her. 'All the same, mind you tell young Lucy not to pull out them electrical wires from the back of the dashboard. Else you and she won't be going anywhere fast!'

'Lucy wasn't with me at the time,' she protested, but he only gave another rumble of laughter before putting down the phone.

Frowning in puzzlement, she didn't have time to think any more about the matter as she heard the toot of a horn. A moment later, her daughter raced into the house as fast as her young legs could carry her.

'Mummy...Mummy! I've had a really *fan-tab-ulous* time!' Lucy cried, throwing her arms about her mother's waist. 'Emily and I saw Father Christmas, and he gave me a lovely present,' she added breathlessly. 'It was terrific—really *wicked*!'

'I gather that's the very latest "in" word, at the moment,' Rose said, smiling at the bemused expression on her friend's face as she handed over Lucy's small suitcase. 'We loved having her and she was as good as gold,' she added, quickly brushing aside Amber's grateful thanks for giving her daughter such a treat. 'I'd love to be able to stop and tell you all about it, but I must get back home. There's a mountain of ironing to be done—and I haven't a clue what I'm going to cook for lunch!'

After waving goodbye to Rose, Amber hurried back into the house, but Lucy was nowhere to be seen. Only the tall figure of Max standing in the kitchen.

'Ah, there you are. Hurry up. It's time we were off.'

'Off where?' she demanded curtly, deeply resenting the sick feeling in the pit of her stomach as she viewed his firmly muscled legs in the tight-fitting, dark blue denim jeans topped by a thick, navy-blue sweater that emphasised his tan. He looked tough, formidable and—alas—so outrageously attractive that she had to swallow hard, fighting to control a mad impulse to leap into his arms. 'Where's Lucy?' she asked anxiously. 'I hope you haven't...'

'Relax! I haven't done anything,' he retorted impatiently. 'I merely suggested that both you and she might like to see my grandmother's old house—or more accurately, what's left of it—followed by lunch in the local pub. Lucy seemed to think that it was a splendid idea. Especially when I promised to help her build a snowman!'

Amber hesitated, longing to tell him to get lost. On the other hand, she knew that he'd already spiked her guns by telling Lucy, and to refuse to go along with his plans would only result in the little girl being disappointed and upset. Besides, like the rest of her neighbours, she'd never been invited to his grandmother's home, since old Lady Parker had been a recluse for the twenty-five years up to her death. The large house was now apparently a pile of rubble. However, she had to admit—privately, to herself— that it might be interesting to see the ruins.

'Well?'

She shrugged. 'Yes... all right. But I'm not sure about lunch. A lot of pubs aren't too keen on letting in young children.'

'That's no problem. I've already phoned up the Red Lion and checked that it's OK. However, don't forget that it's freezing outside, so make sure that you're both well wrapped up,' he added, glancing at her slim figure, clothed in a cream-coloured Aran sweater and tan cords. 'And it might be a good idea to take a thermos of coffee along with us, as well.'

The damned man thinks of everything! she thought gloomily as she finally tracked Lucy down in her mother's side of the house, excitedly telling her grandmother all about her wonderful time in London.

Anxious to assure her mother that they wouldn't be away from the house for too long, Amber was amazed to find the older woman up, dressed and in surprisingly good spirits.

'I'm feeling *much* better, so there's no need to worry about me, dear,' Violet told her with a beaming smile. 'You just run along and enjoy yourselves.'

Puzzled, but at the same time extremely grateful for her mother's sudden return to apparent good health, Amber hurried down to the kitchen, quickly filling a thermos before bundling herself and Lucy into some warm clothes.

Never having seen the old Victorian mansion, Amber had difficulty in imagining how it must have looked in its heyday. After the fire in which Max's grandmother had died, there now remained only a burnt-out shell, many of whose walls had been reduced to rubble, with broken statues and cracked urns lying discarded on the weed-covered terrace overlooking the wooded valley far below. However, most of the outbuildings, garages and stables were in reasonably good shape. As was the orangery.

'Did your grandmother ever grow oranges in here?' Amber asked as she gazed around at what appeared to be a large, elegant and surprisingly warm room.

'No, I shouldn't think so. But since I never met the old dragon, I really haven't a clue.' Max shrugged his broad shoulders. 'I'm far more interested, at the moment, in a hot cup of coffee. Quite frankly,' he added with a grin, 'I never realised that building a snowman would be such hard work!'

'It's harder than it looks,' Amber agreed with a laugh as she looked out of the window at Lucy, who was now busy decorating a decidedly lopsided, squat-looking structure with Max's long woollen scarf.

Despite having been so anxious about the situation, and deeply apprehensive about Max's desire to get to know his daughter, it was a relief to realise that her fears had been completely unfounded. He had treated the little girl very much as he might any other seven-year-old—not only laughing at her terrible jokes, but also laying down very firm, strict instructions to avoid going anywhere near the potentially dangerous ruins of the old house.

'It seems so extraordinary that you never met your grandmother,' Amber said a few moments later, filling their cups with hot liquid from the thermos as he brushed the cobwebs and dirt from two dusty old packing cases. 'Especially since you and your father were living only a few miles away.'

Max sighed and shrugged his shoulders. 'It's a long story, but basically it seems that my grandmother was a lonely, embittered old woman. Her husband had been killed in World War II, and when her only son was killed on the hunting field, she clung like grim death to her sole remaining child—a daughter called Imogen.

'It must have been a stifling, desperately boring life for my poor mother,' he continued, explaining how Lady Parker would never allow her daughter to go anywhere on her own, being deliberately rude and scaring off all her boyfriends, until the poor girl had become virtually a prisoner, clearly destined to spend the rest of her days as an unpaid companion to her elderly mother.'

'But why didn't she just take to her heels and run away?'

'Because she was, by all accounts, a very sweet and
gentle person. She simply couldn't bring herself to be
unkind to anyone—let alone her own mother. And in
any case, by the time Imogen was approaching middle
age, she'd become quite convinced that no one would
ever want to marry her. However, it seems she did
find her religion a great source of help and strength.
Luckily, Lady Parker had no objections to her
daughter visiting the local church in Elmbridge as
often as she liked—which is how she came to meet
my father.'

However, as the story unfolded, Amber was touched
to hear how the Reverend Augustus Warner, a kind
if somewhat absent-minded bachelor in his late forties,
had fallen deeply in love with the unhappy, thirty-
eight-year-old Imogen Parker. 'He wasn't the slightest
bit interested in her mother's wealth, of course,' Max
said, relating how his father had tried to gain his future
mother-in-law's approval for his marriage to Imogen.
But when she had resolutely refused to give the couple
her blessing—even going so far as to forbid her
daughter to ever see the vicar again—Imogen had, at
last, found the courage to defy her mother. 'There
was nothing she could do to stop the wedding, of
course. But the old dragon never forgave her daughter
for "running away" with my father.'

'It seems impossible to believe that *anyone* could
be so cruel and heartless!' Amber exclaimed, shocked
to hear how, when poor Imogen had died after giving
birth to Max some eighteen months later, Lady Parker
had continued to refuse to have anything to do with
either the vicar or her grandson.

As he related the sad story, Amber suddenly gained a fresh insight into how lonely Max must have been as a small child, with no mother to care for him, and an elderly father who'd had no idea how to rear his son. No wonder the boy, brought up by a series of temporary housekeepers, had turned into a wild teenager. She could only think that it was a miracle he hadn't become involved in any really serious trouble.

However, gazing at the man who was sitting across the room from her, Amber was surprised to discover that they'd actually managed to spend some time together in perfect harmony. Was that because today he'd been in a quiet and reflective mood very different from the harsh and aggressive stance he'd displayed last night? It looked as though he was making a conscious effort to control the hard, forceful personality that she knew lay beneath that handsome exterior. Something for which she could only be thankful, she reminded herself quickly, profoundly grateful that Max had made no allusion to the events that had taken place last night.

But it seemed that he had been merely biding his time.

'This appears to be a good opportunity for us to have a quiet talk,' Max said, rising to his feet and strolling over to the window.

'I really don't think so...' she muttered nervously as he waved through the glass at Lucy, who was energetically assembling a large pile of snowballs. 'Besides, it will soon be time for lunch.' She glanced quickly down at her watch. 'So, maybe we ought to...'

'Relax! I don't imagine either of us is in the mood for any more rows or arguments,' he said firmly. 'But since you obviously consider me a double-dealing villain, it seems only fair that you should hear *my* side of the story.'

'There's no need...' she murmured, the rest of what she was going to say being lost as he gave an unhappy bark of laughter.

'There's *every* need.' He brushed a hand roughly through his thick dark hair. 'You have, after all, accused me of behaving with almost criminal irresponsibility by my abandoning a young teenage girl and leaving her to face a traumatic pregnancy without any help or support. Although—God help me!—that last charge *is* unfortunately true,' he added with a heavy sigh.

Amber gave a helpless shrug of her slim shoulders. 'Look, we've been through all this ad nauseam. I realise that I've given you a hard time, and said some horrid things to you, about what happened all those years ago. But that was in the past. We've both now made new lives for ourselves. What's the point in raking it up all over again?'

'The *point*, my dear Amber, is that your version of events does not tie up with mine,' he retorted bluntly, turning to give her a hard, searching look from beneath his dark brows. 'When, before leaving for America to join my uncle, I asked you to be my wife and to wait until I'd made arrangements for you to join me in the States, I meant *every word* of what I said.

'However, until the other day, I had no idea that in the flurry of my departure, I'd omitted to give you my uncle's phone number. All I knew was that we'd arranged for me to contact you on your arrival in London, when you'd have finished packing up your old home in Elmbridge and would know more about your mother's state of health and mind. Are we in agreement so far?'

She shrugged. 'Yes, I suppose so.'

'Right. Now, what you *don't* know is that shortly after I'd landed in the States, my uncle and I were in his car, due to attend a meeting in one of the factories he owned, when we were hit head-on by a large truck. I don't remember anything about the accident. All I know is that I eventually woke up to find myself in hospital with a broken arm, two broken legs and a bad case of concussion. I also learned that I was lucky to be alive—unlike my uncle, who'd been at the wheel of the car and had, unfortunately, been killed outright.

'However,' he continued as she gave an involuntary gasp of horror, 'while I was lucky not to have anything tricky, like amnesia, I did suffer from very intense, sick headaches for a long time after my limbs had healed and I was back on my feet. But that was nothing compared to the headache of trying to run my uncle's business. Although I was his only living relative, I was amazed to learn that he'd recently drawn up a will leaving me everything he owned.'

Max turned his dark head to give her a wry grin. 'As you can imagine, neither the other directors of the firm, nor the workforce, were too thrilled about *that*. And you can't blame them. Weeks seemed to go

by when I felt just so damn tired and ill that I didn't
know how I was going to be able to cope. So, by the
time I got my act together, I was not only having to
work my guts out to prove that I was capable of
running the company—if only to justify the faith
which my uncle must have had in me—but I also
realised that it was over two months since I'd been in
touch with you.'

She gave a helpless sigh. 'If only I'd known about
your accident. But I'd no idea . . .'

'Of course you hadn't,' he agreed swiftly. 'Just as
I had no idea of *your* problems. Believe me, if there
was ever a story of two star-crossed lovers, this is
definitely it!' He began pacing up and down over the
grey flagstones. 'Unfortunately, when I did get around
to phoning you in London, I got your aunt on the
line, thrilled to bits about the news of your forthcoming marriage to Clive Stanhope.'

'Oh, no!'

'Oh, *yes*!' he ground out. 'I was in such a state of
shock that it was some time before I understood what
the old trout was saying. I can still hear her now:
"They're so happy! It's *such* a suitable marriage—
just what her dear father would have wanted,"' he
savagely mimicked her aunt's plummy voice. ' "Clive
is *so* wealthy. Have you ever seen Elmbridge Hall? A
wonderful old house—just perfect for two young
people to start their married life!" And a whole lot
more drivel on the subject of both Clive's wealthy
lifestyle and your past, *very* close friendship.'

'No, that's not true!' she was stung into retorting.
'I hardly knew Clive before he offered to marry me.'

'Not a word about the baby, of course,' Max continued grimly, ignoring her protest. 'For God's sake, Amber! Am I supposed to believe that your aunt was completely blind? Surely she *must* have known that you were pregnant?'

Amber hung her head. 'Yes...well, I suppose she probably did guess the truth,' she mumbled. 'But we never talked about it. She was very old-fashioned and...um...'

'...mightily relieved that her niece was getting married in the nick of time?' Max queried sardonically, pausing in his restless pacing for a moment to throw a searching, steely glance at the clearly unhappy, huddled figure of the girl sitting across the room. 'Well, there's not much more to tell,' he continued bleakly. 'As you can imagine, I went completely off the rails. However, when I eventually sobered up and realised there wasn't much point in drowning my sorrows in wine, women and song, I did the only thing I could—which was to throw myself into work. I developed and expanded my uncle's business, gobbling up many other companies on the way until going public and floating Warner International on Wall Street. Now, all these years later, I've also taken over a large business here in the UK. So, I guess it could be said that my story has a happy ending. Right?'

She nodded silently, not trusting her voice as she tried to come to terms with all that he'd said. It was absolutely shattering to realise that all her preconceived notions, all the unhappy and traumatic events of the past, should turn out to be the result of nothing more than a few unfortunate twists of fate. It seemed almost impossible to believe that a car accident and a missing phone number could be responsible for all the unhappiness of the past eight years.

Amber yawned, leaning back against the padded leather headrest. Goodness knows where Max had got hold of this huge, luxurious vehicle. But she had to admit that with the snow beginning to fall once again, a Range Rover was the perfect vehicle to cope with dangerous icy roads. Which made it all the more peculiar that Max, despite the obviously bad driving conditions, had insisted on taking her out to dinner. Like any other sensible person, she would have preferred to stay indoors by the fire. But Max, as usual, had managed to get his own way.

Turning her head to glare at the man sitting beside her, Amber's frustration at being ordered around was slightly mollified by the sight of a large bruise on his cheek. Good for Lucy! Although the little girl had never intended to hurt him, of course, she reminded herself quickly, recalling how when she and Max had left the orangery, they'd found themselves being pelted by snowballs. It had been an energetic fight, with Lucy—who'd already assembled her ammunition—screaming with laughter as Max had enthusiastically joined in the fun. Unfortunately, when the child had at last managed to score a direct hit on his face, it seemed that a large stone had become accidentally embedded in the snowball.

Although she was reluctant to give him any credit, Amber had to admit that Max had coped very well with the situation. Quickly drying Lucy's tears, he'd explained that it was a well-known hazard of the game, which he, as a veteran of many such fights had fully expected to happen, before suggesting that it was time for lunch. After providing her favourite meal of beef burgers and chips smothered in tomato sauce and, after returning home, playing innumerable childish card games in front of a roaring fire, it was no wonder that Lucy had taken such a shine to 'Mummy's old schoolfriend'. In fact, Amber thought sourly, by the time he'd been persuaded to read her a long bedtime story, it was not surprising that her daughter was beginning to think that Max was the best thing since sliced bread!

Confused by the conflict of emotions in her head, Amber gave a heavy sigh. She knew she ought to be pleased and happy that Lucy and Max were obviously getting on so well together. But she couldn't seem to help resenting their instinctive understanding of one another—or the way in which he seemed to have charmed the socks off her mother. With Violet, who appeared to have taken on a new lease of life, enthusiastically seconding Max's proposal to take her out to dinner, Amber hadn't been able to think of any viable reason for refusing the invitation.

'You're very silent,' Max said, breaking the heavy silence within the car.

'I...er...I'm still not happy about leaving my mother in charge of Lucy,' she muttered nervously, suddenly feeling threatened by the dominant presence of the man sitting so close to her. 'She hasn't been well, and...'

'Nonsense! There's nothing wrong with your mother,' he said crisply. 'In fact, Violet appeared to be in excellent spirits this morning when I told her I was buying your house.'

'You did *what*?'

'As a guest in your home, it would have been extremely bad manners if I *hadn't* seen your mother and also informed her of my plans,' he pointed out blandly. 'Which is why I also felt obliged to ask her for your hand in marriage.'

'Who are you k-kidding?' Amber spluttered furiously. 'I don't believe you've ever felt "obliged" to do anything in the whole of your damn life!' she grated, longing to slap that sanctimonious, holier-than-thou expression from his handsome face. 'You rat! If you've upset her in any way, I'll...'

'Oh, come on!' he gave a sardonic laugh. 'Violet is absolutely thrilled to bits at both being able to remain in the house and the idea of a Christmas wedding. However, I did extract a promise from your mother not to tell anyone. Certainly not until we'd both had an opportunity to discuss the matter with Lucy.'

He's done it again! The wretched man had found yet *another* weapon to coerce her into his insane idea regarding their marriage. Desperately wishing that she could lock herself away in a dark room and scream blue murder, Amber realised that Max now had her well and truly over a barrel. How could she possibly combat both her mother's delight at not having to leave Elmbridge Hall, *and* the fact that Lucy was bound to be thrilled to have a real father at last? On the other hand, how could she bear to marry a man who clearly wasn't in love with her? A man obsessively determined to pursue his mad plans for a Christmas wedding simply to gain parental control over Lucy?

Certain that she was going to disgrace herself by bursting into tears at any minute, she turned her head to stare blindly out of the passenger window. It was only then, as Amber caught a glimpse of an illuminated road sign, that she realised they were travelling along the main road leading to London—something she ought to have recognised long before now, if it hadn't been for the dark winter night and her own heavily depressed state of mind.

'What's going on?' she demanded. 'I thought you were supposed to be taking me out for dinner?'

'You're quite right—I am,' he agreed blandly. 'I merely thought you might like to dine at my apartment in London.'

'You must be out of your mind! Why on earth would I want to go all that way just for a meal?'

'I can give you any number of reasons,' he drawled smoothly. 'Because I thought you might appreciate eating something different from that served in the local restaurants; because my housekeeper is a first-class cook and has promised to leave us a delicious meal in the oven; because I thought it would do you good to get away from Elmbridge for a bit, and because...'

'OK, OK,' she snapped. 'But what about Lucy? My mother is normally a perfectly reliable baby-sitter, but...'

'Calm down,' he retorted firmly. 'Before we left, I told your mother exactly where we were going, and also gave her my phone number in case any problems should arise.'

Totally outraged and incensed at Max's continued interference in her life, Amber's fury intensified as she caught a glimpse, in the headlights of a passing car, of Max's eyes gleaming with unconcealed mockery, and became aware that his broad shoulders were shaking with amusement. But the infuriating man continued to ignore her protests that she wanted to return home, and unfortunately, it wasn't long before she found herself being driven into an under-ground car park beneath a large, modern building overlooking Hyde Park.

'*Good Heavens*!' she exclaimed some minutes later, finding it difficult to maintain her anger as she gazed around the sumptuously furnished sitting room of the penthouse apartment. Her eyes widened at the sight of so many marble columns and the huge floor-to-ceiling window providing a spectacular, panoramic view of the London skyline.

It was an amazing place, she thought, her shoes almost disappearing in the thick pile of a white carpet covering the floor of the large main room, which was decorated with ultra-modern chairs, sofas and glass tables of every shape and size. Staring at the huge, plate-glass windows draped with thick, cream linen curtains, she found herself wondering just how many women had spent time with Max in this opulent, luxurious apartment. Goodness knows, she'd never actually *seen* a male 'love nest', but it didn't take an overheated imagination to realise that this place with its long, black deep leather sofas and enormously large modern paintings of nude women must be the real thing!

'I thought this place might give you a bit of a laugh!' Max said cheerfully as she found herself staring incredulously at an *extremely* rude picture on the wall. 'Unfortunately, I inherited the apartment from a previous managing director of the company—who seems to have had more girlfriends than I've had hot dinners! So, please don't accuse me of having such ghastly, terrible taste, because, quite frankly, I can't wait to move out of here.'

To her surprise, Amber found herself smiling at his lugubrious expression as he gazed around the large room, and almost weak with laughter as later, during dinner, he entertained her with stories about the amorous exploits of his predecessor. 'You wouldn't believe some of the phone calls I've had here,' he grinned. 'I can't make up my mind whether the man was a regular Don Juan—or the Marquis de Sade!'

'I really ought to say I'm sorry for having been such a grouch earlier this evening. Because you were quite right,' she admitted when they were sipping their coffee and brandy in the drawing room. 'That was a really delicious meal—and it's a great treat for me to have the pleasure of eating someone else's cooking.'

'That's a more handsome apology than I deserve,' he told her quietly, falling silent for a moment and buried deep in thought as he stared down at the brandy glass in his hand. 'It wasn't just the shock of seeing Lucy, although, God knows, that left me completely

traumatised for a long time,' he said at last, the raw
bitterness in his voice causing her to look at him
anxiously. 'It was discovering the many years of
financial struggle and the sheer, grinding poverty that
lay behind the seemingly wealthy façade of your
house, which completely threw me for a loop. Even
now, hearing you talk about the "treat" of enjoying
someone *else's* cooking is enough to make me see red.
I really don't think I'll *ever* be able to forgive myself
for allowing you and Lucy to endure such an
experience.'

Wincing as the harsh, savage tones echoed loudly
in the small room, Amber instinctively turned to the
man sitting beside her on the sofa to place a comforting hand on his arm. 'Please, Max, there's no need
to torture yourself like this—or exaggerate my difficulties. Don't you realise that I'm so much luckier
than thousands of other people? At least I've got a
roof over my head,' she pointed out firmly. 'Nothing
to do with my present situation could possibly be regarded as your fault.'

'It may not have been directly my fault,' he said
with a heavy sigh. 'But I do have to take full responsibility for much that has happened to you.
Which is one of the reasons why I'm so determined
to make sure that Lucy has a father, and that both
you and she are financially secure from now on.'

'I appreciate what you're saying—I really do,' she
assured him earnestly. 'But you can be a perfectly
good father *and* provide financially for Lucy without
feeling that you have to marry me. I'll have plenty
enough to live on, once the house is sold. Enough to

buy a small cottage well away from Elmbridge, if need be, so that there won't be any gossip about Lucy's parentage. And of course you can see her—just as often as you like,' she added quickly as he gave a determined shake of his dark head.

'Once you're married to a rich, successful man—who's likely to attract business to the town—you'll find that there will be virtually no unkind gossip.'

'I don't know anything about such matters,' she said, brushing a distracted hand through her golden brown hair. 'But I'm quite sure that money isn't everything in life. It certainly can't buy you happiness, for instance.'

'No. But it can make damn sure that you're unhappy in comfort,' he retorted with a wry, twisted smile.

'My God, how can you be so cynical?' she accused him bleakly, angrily banging her coffee cup down on the low glass table in front of them. 'Is that the sort of marriage you're planning for us? Two people trapped in a thoroughly miserable existence? Surrounded by luxury, and yet not even talking to one another?' she demanded, jumping angrily to her feet. 'Well, I don't want *any* part of it! And I definitely don't want——' She broke off, eyeing him warily as she saw him rise slowly from the sofa and begin moving determinedly towards her.

'I know *exactly* what you want!' he drawled, his mouth twitching in silent humour.

'No, you don't'!' she retorted defiantly as she backed nervously away from his tall figure, her progress abruptly halted as she felt her back jar up against

one of the cold, marble pillars decorating the room.
'I'm no longer that stupid little teenager that you once
knew, Max,' she continued breathlessly, almost hating
the diabolically attractive man gazing down at her,
the hard, sensual gleam in his glittering blue eyes
causing her stomach to clench with sexual tension.
'I'm twenty-six years old and perfectly capable of
realising what you have in mind. Believe me, it's *not*
the right answer.'

'Believe me, it most certainly *is*!' he mocked softly,
taking another step forward.

'No... no, you're quite... quite wrong,' she protested. He was now standing so close to her that she
could see the long, black eyelashes over his gleaming
blue eyes, and the faint flush of arousal beneath the
tanned skin stretched tightly over his high cheekbones
and formidable jawline.

'Isn't it about time you stopped trying to fool
yourself, Amber?' he drawled, raising his hand to run
a finger lightly down the side of her face. 'What's the
point of continuing to deny your own needs and
desires?'

She could feel her heart beginning to pound at the
feel of his soft touch on her skin. 'No, you're quite
wrong about me,' she retorted breathlessly, desperately trying to pull herself together. But it was proving
almost impossible to bring her weak mind under
control, to stop herself trembling in response to the
warmth of the long, muscular thighs pressed against
her own, or to ignore the hand now trailing down over
her neck, gently caressing the hollow at the base of
her throat. 'You're making a great mistake...'

'God knows, I've made plenty of mistakes in my life. But *this* definitely isn't one of them,' he told her with a husky laugh, quickly sweeping her up in his arms and carrying her protesting, wriggling figure along a wide corridor to his bedroom.

'No, Max!' she gasped as he tossed her down on to the huge bed before swiftly trapping her beneath the weight of his strong, hard body. 'Let me go!'

'Stop fighting me,' he growled, the sound of his hoarse voice echoing in her ears as his blue eyes blazed down at the girl lying beneath him. 'It's no good trying to fool yourself, Amber. I *know* you want me as much as I want you. Every kiss . . . every movement of your body betrays that fact. My God, you nearly drove me wild last night! I could almost tangibly *feel* the heat of your desire as you trembled in my arms. Why continue to deny what we feel for one another?' he whispered thickly as his dark head came down towards her.

Once again, from the moment his mouth hungrily claimed her trembling lips, all the past years seemed to vanish as if they'd never been. The stark impact of their mutual desire, the force of his kiss and the hands swiftly pulling off her dress before possessively clasping her full breasts, were a potent reminder of the strong physical bond between them. Even now, as she moaned in protest, there seemed nothing she could do to stop herself from being swept along on a fast, rushing tide of heated desire and passion, helpless against the shivering excitement of his warm fingers moving enticingly over the flimsy barrier of thin silk covering her swollen nipples. And then, as the hard

and angrily demanding pressure of his mouth
softened, his lips and tongue now gently bewitching
and beguiling her senses, she realised that he was right.

It was pointless to deceive herself any longer.
Almost fainting with a tremulous, aching need for his
possession, she knew that this was what she'd
wanted—and had been fighting against with increasing desperation—ever since his return to
Elmbridge. She wanted ... she *needed* to feel his
mouth moving sensually over her lips, the excitement
of the hard muscular body pressed tightly against her
own and the erotic, scorching touch of the hands now
setting fire to her flesh.

Raising his head, his breathing as ragged and un-
steady as her own, Max stared down at her with eyes
that blazed fiercely in the grey light of the unlit
bedroom. 'Tell me, Amber,' he rasped, the hoarsely
demanding, imperative note in his voice causing a
fierce knot of desire to burst into flames in her
stomach. 'Tell me that you want me.'

A deep, helpless shudder rippled through her body,
her arms closing about him, her fingers curling into
his thick dark hair. 'Yes—yes, I want you,' she whispered, oblivious of everything except her long years
of emotional starvation and the driving, desperate
compulsion to surrender to his possession, her desire
and need of him so intense that it was like a deep
physical pain.

Gripped by a primitive force that was completely
beyond her control, she barely heard his low, husky
laugh of triumph as he swiftly removed both his
clothes and hers before tossing her back against the

pillows. They both seemed possessed by a raw, animal
hunger that had been repressed for far too long. Her
emotions spinning wildly out of control, Amber felt
no shame or regret as her hands moved over the strong
contours of his body, feverishly savouring the breadth
of his shoulders, his deep chest and flat stomach, the
taut hard muscles of his thighs, the tanned flesh beneath her fingers so achingly familiar, despite the long
years since she'd last held him in her arms.

If seemed as if Max, too, was possessed by a need
to devour every inch of her bare flesh, the increasingly erotic, sexually explicit touch of his mouth and
hands causing her to feel as though she were on fire,
burning and melting with rampant desire. Overcome
by the dynamic, potent force of her love and need for
him, she cried out loud, the breath rasping in her
throat as she panted for release from the tension that
seemed to fill her whole existence. Absorbed by her
own emotional needs, she barely heard his low, deep
groan at the hard, driving thrust of his body as he
finally entered her, responding to the pulsating rhythm
of his powerful body with a wanton, erotic intensity
that devoured them both, the white-hot heat of their
passion exploding in a shimmering starburst before
they fell shuddering into a deep, dark abyss of mutual
joy and satisfaction.

Later, as they lay warmly and drowsily entwined
together, Amber felt his fingers gently turning her face
towards him. 'It's just as well we're going to be
married in ten days' time,' he murmured with a wry

smile. 'There's no way I'd be able to keep my hands off you for much longer than that!'

'Umm...?' she blinked sleepily up at him. Still dazed by her own frenzied response to his fierce, hungry possession and the overwhelming passion that had flared between them, it was a moment or two before she managed to comprehend exactly what he was saying. 'No...no, we can't possibly...' she muttered wildly as she broke free from his embrace. 'I must go back home...I shouldn't have left Lucy...and there's my mother, too...'

'Relax, darling,' he said huskily, firmly pulling her back into his arms. 'Surely you must realise why I deliberately brought you down here to my apartment in London.'

Not having any idea of what he was talking about, she stared blankly up at him, surprised to see a faint flush of embarrassment spreading over his tanned cheeks.

'Oh, Amber...how can you be so dim?' he groaned. 'Can't you see ... there was no way I could make love to you in your own home without the risk of upsetting or disturbing Lucy, who doesn't yet know that we're to be married. On the other hand, I knew that I'd go stark, staring mad if we didn't make love tonight. Which is precisely why we're here in my bed! And don't worry,' he added quickly. 'I borrowed the Range Rover, so even if the roads are covered in snow, I could guarantee to get you home before breakfast. OK?'

'Of course it's not OK,' she retorted tearfully. 'I...well, I'm grateful for your thoughtfulness. But as far as I'm concerned, this has been a really…really terrible mistake!'

'Making love to you was never a mistake,' he said thickly. 'My one great error was not to have married you before I left for America all those years ago. Which is why I intend to rectify that mistake as soon as possible,' he vowed, his hands sweeping possessively over her trembling, quivering body. 'Because it's you I want—and it's you I'm going to have!'

Amber shivered at the flat, hard, determined note in his voice. All the barriers she'd erected over the years had fallen too fast, too violently, and she was frightened at how clearly she had given herself away. She might love this tough, difficult man, but she had no real clue to his innermost feelings, no certainty that he felt anything for her other than a strong, sexual attraction.

'But…but it won't work. I need more time….' she muttered helplessly, her flesh quivering beneath his dominant touch on her naked body.

'Time for you to think of some puerile, weak excuse? Sorry, Amber, but I'm not feeling that generous,' he drawled with silky menace, his fingers gently brushing the hard, swollen points of her breasts with such a slow, enticing sensuality that it was all she could do not to groan out loud as fierce, wild tremors of pleasure flashed through her body like forked lightning. 'So, you're going to promise—here and now—to marry me in ten days' time. Right?'

Quivering with ecstasy, her senses spinning out of control in a frenzy of delight and excitement beneath the overwhelming mastery of his touch, Amber could

only give a deep, helpless sigh as she abandoned
herself to her fate. 'Yes...' she gasped helplessly before
sinking beneath great waves of overwhelming desire
and passion. 'Yes, Max, I...I'll marry you.'

CHAPTER SEVEN

ALTHOUGH she'd spent some anxious moments wondering how to break the news of her impending marriage, Amber realised that she needn't have worried. Now, four days after agreeing to marry Max, and with only a week to go until the wedding, everyone in the town seemed to be fully aware of what was going on and delighted to hear that the Hall wasn't going to be sold after all.

Everyone, she reminded herself, except 'Gloomy Glover'—clearly regretting the loss of his commission on the sale of her home—and Cynthia Henderson, who'd suddenly decided to leave an assistant in charge of her shop before swiftly departing on a month's cruise around the Caribbean. Unfortunately, today's post had also included a letter from Philip Jackson, who clearly wasn't at all happy about her decision, either.

Sighing as she gazed down at the letter lying on her desk, Amber made yet another attempt to decipher the squiggly writing, which looked more like an inky trail left by a demented spider than heartbroken outpourings full of doom and gloom from the young doctor.

She'd been amazed at the speed with which the news had raced through the small town. When she'd told Max how much she dreaded having to tell everyone, he'd merely grinned. 'Just leave everything to your mother and some of her old cronies. I guarantee that the story will be around Elmbridge and back to you inside twenty-four hours!' He'd been quite right, she acknowledged ruefully, thankful that she'd taken the precaution of telling her own friends first of all. Sally Fraser, for instance, would have been mortally wounded if she hadn't heard the glad tidings from Amber's own lips.

While she could only marvel at how everyone seemed to have swallowed Max's romantic fairy tale lock, stock and barrel, she'd been determined to tell her old friend, Rose Thomas, the truth about her secret love affair in the past and the reasons behind the announcement of her wedding.

'Oh, Amber, I'm *so* happy for you!' Rose had cried joyfully, jumping up from her kitchen table and rushing over to throw her arms about her friend. 'None of us ever guessed that you'd had a romance with Max all those years ago. Or that you were carrying on one during these last few weeks, for that matter! Although, now I come to think about it, I wonder why it never occurred to me that you two would be *perfect* for each other?' She beamed at her friend. 'And what's going to happen about the sale of your house? Are you going to take it off the market?'

'Well, it's no longer for sale, of course, but I expect we'll probably own it jointly,' she explained. 'Actually, I'm feeling a bit overwhelmed at the moment because Max is insisting on paying the full asking price into some sort of investment account for me. He says that he wants to make sure that I always have some private money of my own.'

'How kind and generous. He must be crazy about you!' Rose exclaimed, grinning as the other girl's cheeks flooded with colour.

'I'm not sure...' Amber muttered with a helpless shrug. 'I know that he wants to make sure Lucy has a proper father, but I'm really not certain about anything else. We've got all that past history between us, of course, but it's different now....' Her voice trailed unhappily away.

'Look, whatever took place in the past happened to two young people who've now grown up,' Rose told her firmly. 'You're not the same person you were then, and neither is Max. You've both made mistakes—haven't we all!—but now you've got a chance to start a new life together. And if you think he's marrying you just because he feels a deep sense of responsibility towards Lucy—I reckon you must be out of your mind! Quite frankly, Amber,' she added with a wry laugh, 'Max didn't strike me as someone who'd allow himself to be pushed into doing *anything* he didn't want to. So, my advice is to forget all the unhappiness of the past. It's the here and now that's important, for both you and Lucy.'

'Yes, I know you're right. It's just that it's such a big step, and I can't help being nervous. However, I really don't want anyone else to know the full story,' Amber cautioned her friend. 'Quite apart from anything else, I wouldn't like there to be any gossip about Clive, who was so very good and kind to me.'

'You've no need to worry. I won't breathe a word,' Rose promised quickly.

'Over the years, there were so many times when I longed to be able to tell you everything,' Amber sighed. 'But somehow I just lost my nerve at the last minute. However, for everything to come out now... well, it could be very awkward,' she added quietly. 'Especially as far as Lucy and my mother are concerned.'

'Well, for Heaven's sake, whatever you do, don't tell Sally!' Rose grinned. 'All the same, I do wish that you *had* taken me into your confidence. If only because it can sometimes be helpful to talk over one's problems with a friend. And I know that your life as a single parent can't have been easy.'

'It was really tough at times,' Amber agreed. 'You want to do the very best for your child, but it's basically a no-win situation.'

'Well, I think you've done brilliantly. Especially since you also had to cope with your mother's problems, as well. However, I must say that I've never seen Violet looking so fit and sprightly, while Lucy appears to be over the moon with excitement. I take it that she fully approves of both Max and your wedding plans?'

'That's an understatement! She's totally *thrilled* at the idea of having a real father like all her other friends. On top of which, she and Max don't just look so much alike, they also seem to instinctively understand each other, as well. Quite honestly, I can't think why I got myself into such a state.' Amber smiled and shook her head, remembering how she'd almost

worried herself sick, desperately anxious that her
daughter should be happy with the idea of her
mother's remarriage. But, once again, Max had taken
charge of the situation after Amber, almost trembling
with nerves, had spent a considerable amount of time
alone with the little girl, carefully explaining the plans
regarding their future.

'The fact is, Lucy,' he'd said with a warm smile as
he joined them in the sitting room, 'I've always been
madly in love with your mother. However, she—very
sensibly, I may say—chose to marry your father. Clive
Stanhope was a good, kind, very caring man, and
there's no way I can hope to take his place. So, I'm
not going to even try, OK? On the other hand,' he
added with a grin as the small girl had given him a
cautious nod, 'I think we could have a lot of fun.
There are so many things we can all do together as a
family, which maybe your mother didn't have time
for in the past. Such as the three of us going off,
straight after the wedding, for a Christmas skiing
holiday in Switzerland. Only don't tell anyone, because it's supposed to be a big secret. OK?'

'OK,' Lucy had grinned, obviously pleased to be
trusted to keep such an important item of news to
herself.

'However,' Max had continued more seriously, 'I
reckon that the *most* important thing I have to tell
you is that I promise to do my best to make your
mother very happy.'

Lucy had regarded him silently for a moment.
'Mummy told me that you're a very clever
businessman. Are you *very* rich?'

Max had shrugged his shoulders. 'Yes, I guess I am. But as your mother will tell you, money doesn't necessarily buy happiness. Loving and caring for people is far more important.'

'Well, Mummy needs a new car 'cos the Land Rover is always breaking down. And she ought to have some nice new clothes,' the little girl pointed out firmly. 'Can you afford to buy her lots and lots of *really* glamorous dresses?'

'As many as she wants—and all of them absolutely *dripping* with glamour!' he'd agreed with a grin, ignoring Amber's strangled protest at the down-to-earth, almost mercenary attitude that her daughter seemed to be taking over her mother's proposed marriage.

'And . . . um . . . can I be a bridesmaid?' Lucy asked hopefully.

'Of course!' Max laughed. 'Anything else on your shopping list?'

'Well...did Mummy tell you that I've been wanting a pony of my own for simply *ages*?' Lucy gazed up at him with wide, guileless blue eyes. 'If Mummy is having a new car, will you buy me a pony?'

Almost cringing with shame, Amber had held her breath as Max regarded his daughter blandly for some moments before giving a deep chuckle of amusement.

'No, you crafty, hard-bargaining, artful little girl! I'm not giving you a pony. Not straight away. You'll have to wait until the morning of your eighth birthday,' he'd said firmly, smiling as Lucy had dissolved into a fit of giggles before throwing herself joyfully into his arms.

'It wasn't at all funny at the time. I nearly *died* with embarrassment!' Amber said as her friend laughed at the story of Lucy's bargaining session with her new stepfather.

'Except, well . . . he isn't her stepfather, is he?' Rose pointed out gently. 'I mean . . .' she hesitated, 'isn't it going to be a bit of a problem deciding when and how to tell her that Max really *is* her father?'

'I've been worried about that,' Amber agreed with a sigh. 'Especially as she looks so much like him. However, Max feels that we shouldn't rush into telling Lucy too much, too soon. He seems to think that a warm, loving family life will make the fact that he's her real father more or less irrelevant. I can only hope he's right.'

'I'm sure he is,' Rose had said firmly. 'Just as I'm quite sure that he's the man for you. I was never too happy with the idea of your marrying Philip Jackson. To tell the truth, I always thought he was the sort of person who takes himself far too seriously.'

Her friend was right, Amber realised, grimacing down at the long letter from Philip, still lying reproachfully on the desk in front of her. Having her own doubts and worries about the wisdom of marrying Max, she really didn't need to have them reiterated by anyone else, and she was grateful to be distracted by a telephone call from Rose's husband, David Thomas.

'I just thought I'd give you a ring, Amber,' he barked down the phone, the noise of his busy office clearly audible in the background. 'You remember those house deeds you lent to me . . .?'

'Oh, Heavens! I'd forgotten all about them,' she exclaimed.

'I think you'll be pleased to hear that I've made an interesting discovery. *Very* interesting indeed!'

'Really? What have you found out?'

'Well, maybe I ought to call in and explain it all to you. It's a bit involved—quite complicated, really. But it looks as though there's a chance of saving the Tide Mill.'

'That's terrific!' She smiled down the phone with delight. 'Come on, David, don't keep me in suspense. I want to hear all about it—right now!'

However, by the time she put down the receiver, leaning back in her chair to gaze blindly out of the window, Amber's mind was in a complete whirl.

According to David—whose idea of perfect bliss was delving into dusty historical records—when Clive had sold the old Tide Mill, the sale had only included the building and the land on which it stood. He had *not* sold either the tide pool adjacent to the mill, or the ancient rights and ownership of the spit of land surrounding the tide pool where it jutted out into the river.

'I don't know why Clive didn't include the tide pool in the sale. Although, maybe the builder, who originally bought the old mill, wasn't interested in paying extra for what was nothing more than a huge pond,' David suggested. But, as he'd gone on to explain, the old deeds included an ancient Crown Grant of 1667, made under the great seal of Charles II, which gave the owner of Elmbridge Hall a 'good and perfect title' to the whole of the land enclosing the pool *and* most importantly, the river bed itself.

'I'm sorry to be so dim, David, but I really don't understand what you're talking about. I never knew that anyone could own the land *under* a river. Why would they want to do that?'

'Well, the river is tidal, isn't it? So, maybe in times gone by, there were oyster beds laid in the river beside the pool. That could have been a "nice little earner" for whoever owned Elmbridge Hall at the time.'

'There speaks the accountant!' she laughed. 'But I still don't really understand why that old deed is so important.'

'OK, I know it's complicated. But if you looked at a map of the area, you'd see the old mill on the river-bank, and the land that surrounds the tide pool jutting out into the river like a large U. Now, what this ancient deed proves is that all the land forming the outline of the U is still owned by you—and you also own the river bed, which lies between the pool and the other side of the river. I've checked up with a friend in the County Record Office,' he added, his voice crackling with excitement. 'He tells me that if you own the land around the pool *and* the land under the river as far as the river-bank opposite, you are entitled to demand a licence fee of anyone wanting to tie up their boat on to your land.'

'You mean...' Amber frowned as she tried to concentrate on what he was saying. 'You mean, anyone can sail up and down the river, but if they want to come ashore anywhere on my land, they have to have my permission to do so?'

'Got it in one!' David agreed crisply. 'Moreover, since you own the river bed itself, no one can build moorings or drive piles into the earth beneath the river. Which is going to be one big headache for Suffolk Construction, right? Because they may own the Tide Mill, but unless you sell them the pool, the land surrounding it *and* your rights to the river bed, they haven't a hope in hell of building their marina!'

'Wow! I can't wait to tell Rose the good news,' she laughed before realising that she would soon no longer be the sole owner of Elmbridge Hall. 'I'll have to tell Max what you've discovered, although I'm sure he'll be as pleased as I am to hear the news. He's working in London this week, but as I'm going down to do some shopping and then join him for lunch on Friday, I'll be able to tell him all about it. However, don't you think that we ought to let the people at Suffolk Construction know about the old deed?' she added tentatively. 'It does seem a bit unfair to leave them completely in the dark.'

'Yes, you're right,' he agreed. 'I haven't a clue who actually owns the firm. But maybe John Fraser can help? As a solicitor, he's bound to know how to go about finding out that sort of thing. Sorry...I'll have to go,' David had added hurriedly as the background noise in his office suddenly increased in volume. 'I'll give you a ring as soon as I have any more information. Bye.'

'I wish you'd both stop yakking away about the boring old Tide Mill!' grumbled Sally as she helped herself to another cup of tea.

'But that's the whole point of this meeting,' Rose pointed out as she passed around a plate of chocolate biscuits. 'We have to decide whether we're going to close down the committee now that Suffolk Construction can't build their new marina. Or whether we should wait for a while and see what happens.'

'Yes, well...you're right,' Sally agreed with a shrug. 'But, quite frankly, I'm *far* more interested in hearing about the plans for Amber's wedding. You haven't told us what sort of dresses you and Lucy are going to wear.'

'That's because I haven't bought them yet,' Amber grinned, still feeling slightly light-headed after yesterday's phone call from Rose's husband, David.

It seemed almost impossible to believe that everything in her life was suddenly coming up roses. When she recalled just how terrified she'd been at the prospect of Max's return to Elmbridge only a few weeks ago, it was really quite extraordinary the way all her problems appeared to have melted away. It wasn't just her forthcoming marriage to Max in a few days' time—which meant being able to stay in her old home, and which had led to Lucy's joy and happiness at the prospect of gaining a stepfather—but now, thanks to Rose's husband examining those old deeds, it was almost certain that they would be able to save the Tide Mill, as well.

'David said that he's trying to discover who owns Suffolk Construction. But as so many companies have been gobbled up by huge conglomerates these days, it may take him some time,' Rose warned her friends.

'I hope you're not going to try and buy any wedding outfits in Cynthia Henderson's boutique,' Sally demanded, refusing to be sidetracked in her determined pursuit of the latest up-to-date news on Amber's marriage. 'That assistant she's left to run the shop is absolutely *hopeless*!'

'No,' Amber shook her head. 'The sort of clothes Cynthia sells in her shop were always far too flashy for me. I'm going down to London tomorrow, to meet Max for lunch and to do some shopping. I'd thought I might find a suit or...'

'A dress and matching coat would be a better choice, especially since it's freezing cold at this time of year,' Sally wisely pointed out. 'And don't forget that the heating system in the church is always breaking down. You don't want to spend the next two weeks trying to recover from a nasty dose of flu. By the way,' she added casually, 'exactly where *are* you planning to go on your honeymoon?'

Amber laughed. 'Give me a break, Sally! If I tell you, everyone else in Elmbridge will know all about it in five seconds flat!'

'How can you say that? I'd never tell *anyone*,' her friend assured her earnestly, pointedly ignoring Rose's loud snort of amusement and disbelief. 'Are you going somewhere nice and warm, like the Caribbean? You could get a wonderful tan, and...' she paused as David Thomas entered the kitchen.

'Hello, darling. You're home early.' Rose smiled over at her husband before frowning as she noted the slightly apprehensive, worried expression on his face. 'What's wrong? Is everything all right at the office?'

'The office is fine, no problem,' he assured her, coming over to help himself to a cup of tea. 'I didn't know...I didn't realise that you were both here.' He turned to give Sally and Amber a strained smile.

'We were just discussing what you'd discovered in my old deeds,' Amber said. 'However, I think it's probably time we left. Just lately, I seem to be spending more of my life in Rose's kitchen than I do in my own home!'

'There's no need to go,' he assured her quickly. 'I just popped in to see Rose for a moment.'

'Have you had a chance to find out who owns Suffolk Construction?' his wife asked. 'We realise that it may take some time, of course, but——' She broke off as he turned his head to give her a quick glance of warning. 'What is it? It's something to do with the old mill, isn't it?'

'Well...er...I don't suppose it's all that important. We can always talk about it later,' he muttered evasively.

'Come on, David. If what's worrying you concerns the Tide Mill, you can't leave us in the dark,' Rose told her husband impatiently. 'I think you'd better hurry up and let us know the worst.'

'Yes, I suppose so,' he sighed, pulling up a chair and sitting down at the table. 'Although it's not a *major* problem, of course. Just a bit awkward, if you see what I mean?'

Rose groaned. 'No, we don't know what you mean. So, for Heaven's sake, get to the point!'

'Well, there's definitely no problem with the deeds,' he told Amber. 'At the moment, you really do own

all rights to the land and the river bed, as I told you
on the phone yesterday.'

'What do you mean by "at the moment"?' Sally
queried sharply. 'Surely she either does or she doesn't
own the damn things. I've never heard of any deeds
with a time limit on them—not ones dating back to
1667.'

'You're quite right,' he agreed. 'But don't forget
the deeds go with the house. So, there's no problem
while Amber has sole ownership of Elmbridge Hall.
However, when she marries Max, I understand that
he's either buying the house outright from her, or they
are going to share the tenancy.' He turned to Amber.
'Is that right?'

'Yes, I suppose so. We haven't really had much time
to sort it out.' She shrugged. 'Why should it matter
one way or another?'

David hesitated for a moment. 'Well, I don't
know...it just seems a bit odd. You see, I can't
understand why Max hasn't told you that it's *he* who
owns Suffolk Construction.'

'*What*?'

'I don't believe it!'

'You must be kidding.'

'Hang on!' David protested above the loud excla-
mations of shock and horror that had greeted his
statement. 'It's only a small problem. We're not
exactly talking about the end of the world!'

'He's right. There's bound to be a simple reason
why Max hasn't told anyone,' Rose said firmly,
putting an arm about Amber's dazed, trembling
figure. 'But, first of all, David, I think you'd better

tell us how you discovered that Max owns Suffolk Construction. Are you *quite* sure that you haven't made a mistake?'

He shook his head. 'It was Sally's husband, John Fraser, who told me when I asked him to do some digging and find out the owners of the construction firm. From what I gather, it seems that he's been looking after Max's business interests here in Elmbridge for some time. For instance, he arranged the appointment of the present manager, a Mr Cruickshank, and . . .'

'John never said a thing about it to *me*!' Sally protested. 'I'd have told you straight away, if I'd known that Max owned the company.'

'Hmm, yes, I'm quite sure you would have,' Rose agreed, having no doubts about exactly *why* her friend's husband, not wishing the news to be broadcast far and wide, had remained silent on the subject.

'Is it all to do with his grandmother's estate?' asked Sally. 'Was she the original owner of the firm?'

'No, I don't think so,' David said slowly. 'From what John said, it appears that Suffolk Construction was taken over some time ago by a European company that, in turn, was recently taken over and absorbed into Max's firm, Warner International.'

'I'm sure that there's a very simple answer,' Rose told them firmly, throwing a worried, sideways glance at Amber, who was still sitting frozen in her seat, her face ashen with shock as she stared blindly down at the kitchen table.

'Yes—but what?' asked Sally, frowning with bewilderment before bluntly putting into words the unspoken question in the forefront of everyone's mind.

'I mean...Max couldn't *possibly* be marrying Amber to get hold of her house deeds, so that Suffolk Construction can go ahead and build their marina...could he?'

It was a cold, damp, dismal day; the streets of London were even more crowded than usual with people intent on last-minute Christmas shopping, the air thick with exhaust fumes and noisy with the incessant honking of cars, buses and taxis.

Amber had never particularly cared for life in the big city. But she'd forced herself to get the train down to London this morning, fully intent on telling Max *exactly* what she thought of his despicable behaviour. Luckily, she wouldn't have to beard him in his office, since she knew that he was working at home this morning before being due to meet her for lunch at an expensive restaurant in Mayfair. Well, that was a lunch that wouldn't now be taking place, she told herself grimly, impatiently tapping her feet as her taxi was reduced to crawling through the heavy traffic.

Following a sleepless night, mainly spent pacing up and down over her bedroom floor, she had slowly progressed from a state of complete and utter shock to one of boiling rage and fury. How *dare* Max make use of her for his own evil and nefarious plans? The devious rat had obviously sweet-talked his way back into her life—and her heart—with only one aim in mind: to further his own lousy business interests!

Now the scales had fallen from her eyes—she could see it all! He'd clearly had *no* intention of marrying her—not when he'd first called with Mr Glover to look at her house. It was now obvious that Max had merely intended to buy the property in order to gain access to her deeds. And it didn't take a very high IQ to realise exactly *why*, after seeing Lucy, he'd suddenly come up with the idea of marriage. All that business about the little girl needing a father had been nothing but *hogwash*! Amber had told herself furiously. It was obviously her daughter's startling resemblance to Max that had immediately changed his plans. After all, since he had already made arrangements to return to Elmbridge—a fact that he'd freely admitted—he couldn't afford a scandal. And there most certainly *would* have been plenty of scandal and gossip once everyone realised—as they were bound to do sooner or later—that Lucy was his illegitimate daughter. Definitely *not* a good idea for someone who was intending to become a pillar of the local business and social community, Amber thought savagely, almost kicking the door open as her taxi came to a halt outside the large modern apartment block overlooking Hyde Park.

Waiting for the lift to take her up to the top floor, Amber couldn't seem to stop herself shaking with tension. In fact, ever since learning of Max's vile treachery yesterday afternoon, she hadn't been able to think straight—or prevent her limbs and body trembling as if in the grip of some raging fever. 'It's just shock. It will soon wear off,' Rose had told her, clearly worried about letting the stunned, dazed girl

drive the few miles back to Elmbridge Hall. But
although her friends had been very kind, their distress and sympathy with her plight had left her desperately anxious for the sanctuary and shelter of her
own home.

It wasn't that she didn't care about the old Tide
Mill because, of course, she did, Amber told herself
as the lift swept her upwards at breakneck speed, towards the penthouse suite on the top floor of the large
building. It was the overwhelming humiliation and
embarrassment of being such a credulous fool that
she found so hard to bear. Unfortunately, it was no
good trying to blame anyone else for the catastrophic
situation in which she now found herself. It was *she*,
overcome by her own weak, starved emotions and
Max's devastating attraction, who was responsible for
raising the false hopes of both her mother and
daughter. Poor Violet would now undoubtedly lapse
back into her deeply depressed state of mind. And as
for Lucy...? Amber almost whimpered aloud at the
thought of having to deal such a dreadful, crushing
blow to her young daughter's joy and happiness at
the prospect of having, at long last, a father of her
very own.

'Hello, darling, I wasn't expecting to see you until
much later this morning,' Max said as he opened the
front door of his apartment.

It was acutely dismaying to find herself almost
weakening at the sight of Max's lean figure in the
casual, slim-fitting dark trousers, his broad shoulders
covered by a soft, black cashmere sweater over an
open-necked shirt. Just a glance at his tall, lithe body

was enough to make her legs wobbly, her stomach feeling as though it were full of butterflies. Someone should arrange to have him locked up and then throw away the key, she told herself grimly. Because this man was clearly nothing but a damn menace to the whole female population!

'What's brought you here so early?' He raised a quizzical dark eyebrow. 'Have you been on a spending spree and run out of money?'

'No, I haven't run out of money. And, if I had, I certainly wouldn't ask *you* for any,' Amber retorted grimly.

'So, what's the problem?' he murmured smoothly, leading her across the well-polished, shiny parquet flooring of the large hall. 'I'm sorry that I've been rather tied up lately. But we'll soon be able to spend plenty of time together. I'm really looking forward to Christmas.'

'Well, I'm glad at least one of us has something to look forward to! Unfortunately, it won't be either Lucy or myself.'

'Really?' he drawled, his dark brows drawing quickly together in a frown as he registered the sharp, acidic note in her voice. 'Well, maybe I can change your mind. Because, while this apartment is hopeless, I'm still going to need an occasional base in London. So, I was hoping that we'd have time this afternoon to look at some houses that are for sale. They all have large gardens, which I thought would be perfect for Lucy to play in whenever she's down here.'

'You can look at what you like. I couldn't care less one way or another.'

'OK, let's have it,' he shrugged. 'You're obviously upset about something. Although I can't think what—other than the fact that I do seem to have been heavily immersed in business lately.'

'I don't give a damn about your business!' she grated angrily, her fury and resentment returning with a vengeance as she gazed at his tall figure, now lounging casually against one of the marble pillars in the room, his glinting blue eyes regarding her with some amusement. 'Although that's the reason why I'm here, of course,' she continued. 'I just wanted to tell you, face to face, that you can forget any idea of marrying me—because I wouldn't touch you with a ten-foot bargepole!'

'Don't be such an idiot!' he laughed. 'You're just suffering from pre-wedding nerves. I've now got hold of the special licence for our marriage next week, and...'

'Didn't you hear what I said? I told you to forget it!' she snarled. 'And you can also forget any idea of getting hold of my house, as well. Which—as we both know—will rule out any chance of you making yet more millions out of Suffolk Construction.'

'What in the hell are you talking about?'

'Oh, come on, do me a favour!' She gave a shrill, high-pitched laugh. 'Unless they own the deeds of my house, Suffolk Construction hasn't a cat in hell's chance of being able to build the new marina in Elmbridge, right? And *who* owns Suffolk Construction? *Who* persuaded this stupid, gullible fool that he wanted to marry her, so that he could buy her house *and* lay his hands on the deeds? Well—

surprise, surprise!—it's clever Mr Warner. Only I'm afraid it turns out that he wasn't *quite* clever enough,' she added savagely as he straightened up, regarding her with a dangerous gleam in his suddenly hard, blue eyes.

'So, you can forget your precious marina *and* that rotten, bogus marriage you've so carefully arranged,' she continued venomously. 'You can also forget *any* idea of getting your hands on Lucy. Because I don't care if I have to spend my whole life in court! I'll never, *never* let you get your slimy hands on her.'

'That's quite enough!' he thundered angrily, striding over the thick carpet towards her. 'You must be having a brainstorm! I don't know what the hell you're talking about.'

'Can you deny that you own Suffolk Construction?' she yelled angrily.

'No, of course not. Why should I?' He came to a halt, placing his hands on her shoulders as he frowned down into her blazing green eyes. 'God knows, it's only a tinpot little company, going nowhere fast. Why should you be interested in it one way or another?'

'Why indeed?' She glared defiantly up at him, refusing to be intimidated by the superior height of the man looming over her. 'Except that I've *now* discovered the truth about that "tinpot little company" of yours.'

'Oh, really?' he drawled coldly.

'Yes, *really*!' she lashed back, desperately trying to control the tears that threatened to fall at any moment. 'I know all about your wicked plans. So you can forget any idea of a wedding, or of buying my house, *or* the effort of having to pretend to be the stepfather of the year! And . . . and what's more——'

But she didn't have a chance to finish what she was saying, as he propelled her swiftly towards a pair of deep leather armchairs.

'OK, that's it!' he said sternly, pushing her down into a chair before seating himself firmly in the other. 'Now, I want you to take a deep breath and tell me— as calmly as possible, please—exactly what has been going on since I left Elmbridge.'

'Why should I?' she glared at him tearfully. 'You know it all anyway.'

'I know *nothing*!' he ground out savagely through clenched teeth. 'Only that you seem to have flipped your lid, and are apparently accusing me of a quite ridiculous, crazy scheme, which sounds more like something dreamed up by Hollywood than real life. So, get on with it, Amber. And it had better be good!' he added with grim warning. 'Because I'm sick and tired of always being cast as the villain of the piece, as far as you're concerned.'

Haltingly at first, and then speeding up her narrative as he clicked his fingers with terse impatience, she told him about David Thomas's discovery of both the ancient deed and Max's connection with Suffolk Construction. 'I . . . I nearly died with humiliation when Sally pointed out the truth,' she gulped, raising a trembling hand to brush the weak tears from her eyes. 'I couldn't . . . I couldn't believe just what a stupid fool I'd been.'

'I certainly won't disagree with *that* diagnosis!' He gave a harsh bark of angry laughter before slowly rising to his feet and pacing up and down over the white carpet. 'OK, I'll agree that the story you've outlined would make a great movie,' he said at last. 'There's only one problem. How long have you known about this ancient Crown Deed?'

'I only heard about it when David phoned two days ago.'

'Right. And how long has *he* known about this mysterious document?'

'I...I'm not sure,' she muttered. 'He only said that he'd discovered it buried amongst my house deeds.'

'Well, that's very interesting,' Max drawled, walking slowly towards her. 'So, maybe you can tell me how in the blazes *I*—who only returned to this country a few months ago after spending the past eight years in the United States—was supposed to have discovered the deed?

'It would obviously take some time to lay my evil, wicked plans,' he pointed out grimly as she gazed open-mouthed up at him, her brain in a total whirl. 'So, tell me, where and how did I manage to discover such a vital piece of information? Especially when David Thomas, who apparently prides himself on his local knowledge, has only just discovered the damn thing?

'Don't worry, Amber, it's only a small, technical hitch,' he added with cruel sarcasm as she stared at him in dawning horror, the blood draining from her face as she slowly began to comprehend the truth behind his remorseless, logical questions. 'I'm quite sure that your totally overwrought, fertile imagination can come up with an answer. Maybe I hired

James Bond to secretly investigate your house deeds, just in case they might contain something interesting? Or, did I persuade the little green men from Mars to...'

'*Oh, God* ...!' she groaned, gazing at him for one long, grief-stricken moment before covering her face with trembling hands, her slim body shaken by a storm of tears, weeping her heart out both because of her own stupidity—and for the certain loss of the one and only man she'd ever loved.

CHAPTER EIGHT

'WHAT an idiot you are, my darling!'

'I . . . I know . . .' she cried, her tears increasing as she felt a warm hand gently stroking her hunched shoulders. 'I know that you'll *never* be able to forgive me for being so . . . so *incredibly* stupid. . . .'

'Oh, yes, I think I probably will,' he murmured, his blue eyes gleaming with amusement as he bent down to tenderly gather her sobbing figure up into his arms before carrying her out of the room and down a long corridor.

'Where . . . where are you taking me?' she muttered, burying her tear-stained face in the warm curve of his shoulder.

'Where do you think?' he demanded with a husky laugh as he entered his bedroom, lowering her gently down on to the enormous bed.

'Oh, no! We can't possibly . . .'

'Don't give me any of that nonsense, Amber,' he growled. 'Trying to persuade you to marry me has been—without a shadow of doubt—one of the most difficult and exhausting tasks I've ever had to face. It's only because I love you so much that I've kept on banging my head against what has so often seemed like a brick wall.'

'You...you really *do* love me?' she whispered, gazing incredulously up through her wet, spiky eyelashes at the man towering over her. 'But I thought...'

'Of course, I do, you stupid woman!' he ground out with exasperation, impatiently brushing a hand through his thick, dark hair as he sat down on the bed beside her. 'And now, after putting me through the wringer this morning, I have every intention of stripping off that boring tweed suit you're wearing. Because it's definitely about time that you soothed my injured feelings!'

'But, Max, we can't!' she gasped, adding quickly as he glared ferociously at her, 'It's only eleven o'clock in the morning, for Heaven's sake!'

'Oh, God! Who cares whether it's midday—or midnight?' he breathed, roughly pulling her into his arms, fiercely moulding her trembling body to his strong, lean figure with an urgency that made the blood race in her veins.

The musky, masculine scent of his cologne filled her nostrils as his lips fastened urgently on hers, his kiss deepening with possessive force as her soft, helpless moans of pleasure and the warm, yielding response of her slim figure provoked his increasing ardour. There was a desperate hunger in his hands as he swiftly removed her clothes, quickly peeling away his own and clasping her naked form to his hard masculine body, his powerful frame shaking with the force of an urgent, passionate intensity barely under control.

'I love you. I've never stopped loving you—however hard I tried to do so,' he murmured thickly against her soft skin, his lips trailing down over her breasts, provoking helpless gasps and moans of pleasure as his mouth closed over first one swollen nipple and then the other. 'You belong to me—and I'm *never* going to let you go. Never, ever again!'

His hoarse voice was almost the last thing she heard as she sank beneath the fierce tidal waves of overwhelming passion and desire. Feverish tremors of delight shook her body, each lingering caress, each sensual and erotically intimate touch making her ache with the desperate intensity of her need for his possession. Trembling with ecstasy as he placed his hands beneath her, parting her quivering thighs and lifting her up towards him, she was unaware of crying out in a wild, almost inhuman voice as she arched to meet the hard, powerful thrusts of his body. Their driving hunger and need forging them together as they became one flesh and one soul; the universe seeming to explode about them in brilliant, searing fragments of fiery light and heat.

'But, darling, surely you *must* have known how I felt about you?' he murmured softly as she lay curled within the warmth and shelter of his arms. 'How could you have doubted my love? Why else would I want to marry you?'

'But, I . . . I thought it was mainly because of Lucy. That you wanted to look after and provide for her. It wasn't long before I finally realised that I was madly in love with you, of course. But I was so confused about what you felt towards me that I simply wasn't able to think straight. Otherwise, I'd never have leapt to all the silly, wrong conclusions about that awful deed.'

'Oh, my love,' he gave a low, soft laugh. 'You're such an idiot!'

'I know,' she agreed sadly. 'I can't believe that I've been *so* stupid. But when David Thomas mentioned the name of your manager in Elmbridge as being a Mr Cruickshank, and I remembered you talking to someone of that name on your·mobile phone in the car—well, it all seemed to make some kind of terrible sense. That, and the fact that you and John Fraser were obviously involved in business together...' Her voice trailed unhappily away.

'It's all right, darling,' he murmured tenderly, gathering her closer to his hard, naked body. 'The misunderstanding wasn't all your fault. Because, while I can promise you that I *didn't* have anything to do with that deed, I haven't been entirely straight on the matter of my business affairs in Elmbridge.'

'What do you mean?'

'Well, when I took over the large firm in London, it was some time before I discovered that it included a lame-duck company, Suffolk Construction, that was planning to build a marina in Elmbridge. However, I soon realised that there was a considerable amount of local feeling about the plans, and so I decided to put everything on hold until I'd found out the true facts of the case. I reckoned people might talk to me more openly if they *didn't* know I was the owner.'

'Yes, well...I can see that makes sense,' she acknowledged. 'All the same, I do wish that you'd at least told *me* the truth. I'd never have got myself into such a stupid muddle, or made such a fool of myself, if I'd known what was going on.'

'I see now that I should have trusted you,' he agreed. 'But although finding that I'd become the owner of Suffolk Construction was a complete accident of fate, it did give me a good and valid reason to hang around the neighbourhood, quite apart from the fact that I'd suddenly inherited my grandmother's estate. And that's what I needed. Because I was quite determined—once I learned that Clive had been killed in a car accident some years ago—to return to the town and, somehow, renew my relationship with you.'

'But you can't have intended to marry me? Not before you discovered that Lucy was your daughter?'

He gave a heavy sigh. 'I honestly don't know *what* I intended to do. For years I'd burned with resentment at the way you'd thrown me over—and for a man whom I thought of as an idle, rich, landowning ne'er-do-well. Yes... yes, I know,' he added quickly as she stirred restlessly in his arms. 'I now realise the truth of what happened in the past. But when I returned to Elmbridge, I...well, I guess I must have had some sort of half-baked idea in the back of my head. Not of carrying out any kind of punishment or revenge, of course. But, somehow, hoping that you were now bitterly regretting not having married me.'

'Oh, Max!' she murmured, raising herself up on one elbow to gently brush the damp curls from his brow. 'That sounds almost as foolish as some of the silly things I thought, and did.'

He gave a rueful laugh, his cheeks flushing beneath her fond smile. 'Frankly, darling, I'm deeply ashamed at having to confess anything quite so pathetic and juvenile. However, when I discovered the truth—that

far from living in rich, glamorous surroundings, you
were existing virtually on the poverty line—I quickly
realised that I had an opportunity to grab you for
myself at last! Unfortunately, my courtship proved to
be a very difficult and tricky undertaking.'

'*Courtship*...?' Amber exclaimed, gazing at him
with incredulity for a moment before falling back
against the pillows, her body shaking with laughter.
'*What* courtship? I've had nothing but dire threats
and menace from the first moment we met—and well
you know it!'

'Yes, you have a point,' he grinned. 'But I don't
think you realise just how difficult it was to try and
get close to you. I wasn't even entirely sure how much
you still cared for me—although I knew from your
response to my kisses that we were still strongly attracted to one another. And while you may laugh
about my so-called courtship, just trying to get myself
through the door of Elmbridge Hall nearly stumped
me,' he added with a sigh. 'In fact, I'm afraid to say
that it was only when I resorted to underhand
methods, by pulling out the electric wiring of your
car, which you'd left unattended in the High Street,
that I finally managed to inveigle my way into your
house.'

'Do you mean to say...?' She glared at him
indignantly.

'Yes, I'm afraid so!' he admitted with a grin. 'I was
worried about that handsome doctor, Philip Jackson.
I'd already heard from John Fraser that he was keen
on you. But when I saw him kissing you in the middle
of the High Street, I knew that I was going to have

to move damn fast,' Max added grimly. 'I had to make
sure that I'd got you well and truly committed to *me*,
before that guy had a chance to propose marriage.'

'Actually, he'd already asked me to marry him—
about six months ago,' she murmured, secretly thrilled
to the core to learn that Max had been jealous of the
young doctor.

'And...?'

'And—nothing,' she replied quickly as his arms
tightened possessively about her. 'I always knew that
he wasn't the right man for me.'

'What about Clive?'

She blinked at him in puzzlement. 'But I've already
told you about him. You know all about our
marriage.'

'Er...no, not quite,' he murmured. 'Don't forget
that before I actually saw Lucy, I was well aware of
the fact that you had a young daughter. I naturally
assumed that Clive was her father. That you and he...'

'Oh, no,' she said quickly, her cheeks flushing beneath his steady gaze. 'Clive and I...we never...we
didn't...' She took a deep breath. 'There's never been
anyone else. I know it sounds feeble, but...but you're
the only man who's ever made love to me.'

'Oh, *darling*!' he groaned. 'You wouldn't *believe*
just how jealous I've been of that poor guy. I knew
I had no right...and God knows I'll always be so
grateful to him for looking after you, but...' His
mouth claimed hers in a deeply possessive, passionate
kiss that seemed to last for ever. When he at last let
her go, she lay flushed and breathless in his arms.
'My sweet one,' he whispered. 'I love you with all my

heart—which you captured for all time eight years ago.
And while I can't say that I've lived like a monk since
we parted, I can promise you that I've never become
seriously involved with anyone else.'

'Oh, yes? What about Cynthia Henderson?' she
teased.

'Well...' he paused, grinning down at her as he
pretended to give the matter some considerable
thought. 'I was pleased to note that you showed
definite signs of being extremely jealous when she
threw herself all over me at the party in the Assembly
Rooms.'

'Now just a minute!' Amber protested. 'I wouldn't
bother getting *too* swollen headed about that fact, if
I were you. Because, given half a chance, Cynthia can
be relied upon to leap into just about *anyone's* bed!'

'Hmm...that's interesting. I've always been very
partial to voluptuous ash-blondes,' he drawled pro-
vocatively, laughing as she quickly rose to the bait,
angrily thumping his chest with her clenched fists. 'But
what I *really* can't resist is a girl with tawny hair and
green eyes, who's going to be my wife in a few days'
time. Right?' he demanded huskily, rolling over to
trap her beneath his powerful body.

'Oh, *yes!*' she breathed ecstatically as he softly
brushed his mouth over her trembling lips. 'You are
absolutely, one hundred per cent *right!*'

'Doesn't Amber look simply *lovely!*' Sally murmured, staring across the room at the newly married
couple, clearly oblivious of the photographer's flash-
bulbs as they gazed deep into each other's eyes.

'Yes,' Rose sighed, wiping away a tear. 'I don't think I've ever seen her looking so beautiful—or so happy.'

'I thought that this was going to be a quiet wedding with only one or two guests,' Sally said as she gazed around the large, oak-panelled walls of Elmbridge Hall. 'But as far as I can see, they must have invited at least half the town to the wedding!'

Rose laughed. 'According to Max, his first mistake was to give Violet Grant a blank cheque as far as expenditure on the wedding was concerned. And his second major error was not checking the number of people on the guest list before Violet had issued all the invitations!'

'Well, it's no secret that Amber's mother is a bit dotty. Sometimes not quite "all there", if you know what I mean,' Sally murmured quietly as Violet, wearing a very smart lilac chiffon-and-lace dress, smiled vaguely at them from across the room. 'But you have to admit that she's always had wonderful taste. I don't think that I've ever seen this house looking so lovely. In fact,' she added confidentially, 'I'm told that the bill for those magnificent flower arrangements came to many *hundreds* of pounds. And goodness knows what Amber's gorgeous coat and dress must have cost—it doesn't bear thinking about!'

'Hmm...' Rose murmured, well aware of *exactly* how much had been spent on the bride's outfit from one of the top fashion houses in London.

'I know my darling bride-to-be,' Max had told her a few days before the wedding. 'She's so used to not spending anything on herself that she'll buy the first thing she thinks is even vaguely suitable. So, I want you—as her oldest and dearest friend—to make sure that both she and Lucy are dressed up to the nines. Money is no object,' he added firmly, scribbling a note on the back of one of his business cards. 'Just tell them to send the bill to me.'

It had taken a considerable amount of arm twisting and plain speaking, but Rose had eventually persuaded her friend that she owed it to Max—if not for any other reason—to look her very best at the wedding. And once they'd been shown the simple but beautifully cut, pale cream woollen dress with its matching cloak and hood, lined in cream-coloured fur, Amber had immediately agreed that it was the perfect choice.

'I wish it was *real* fur,' Sally was saying. 'Goodness knows, Max can afford it.'

'But Amber wouldn't wear it,' Rose retorted, knowing that her friend shared her own feelings of revulsion at the slaughter of innocent wild animals. However, before they could disagree any further on the merits, or otherwise, of the anti-fur lobby, Lucy danced up to them, almost beside herself with excitement.

'Look at me, Aunt Rose! Don't I look *stu-pen-dous*!'

'You certainly do!' she laughed as the little girl twirled around in front of her. Indeed, Lucy was almost heartbreakingly lovely in her cream silk dress, with its lace-trimmed petticoats edged in palest pink, matching the wide sash about her waist and the large bow in her hair. 'In fact, I thought you made a really beautiful bridesmaid.'

'As beautiful as Mummy?'

'Well...almost—but not quite,' she murmured, gazing misty-eyed at the radiant glow on Amber's lovely face.

'But my new daddy is *easily* the most beautiful man,' Lucy said firmly before dashing across the room.

'She's so right—it's no contest!' Sally grinned, watching as the child's handsome new stepfather laughingly swept the little girl up in his arms. 'Incidentally, I can't help thinking that it's lucky Lucy looks so much like Max,' she added, thoughtfully viewing the two dark, curly heads pressed closely together. 'It makes them seem more of a real family somehow.'

'Umm...but don't forget that Clive had blue eyes and dark hair exactly the same colour as Lucy's,' Rose pointed out as calmly. 'Not as curly, of course. But then, most children's hair tends to grow straighter as they become older, doesn't it?'

'Yes, of course, you're quite right,' Sally agreed, immediately dismissing the vague, very faint question mark that had just floated through her mind. 'I sometimes think children are like puppies, who often mature into dogs that closely resemble their owners. So, I expect that will happen with Lucy and Max. Because anyone with half an eye can see that she absolutely *adores* her new father.'

Sighing with relief at having successfully deflected Sally's inquisitive nose for gossip, Rose quickly

changed the subject. 'I know that he was very unhappy about losing Amber to Max, but I'm so pleased
that Philip Jackson accepted an invitation to the
wedding.'

'He was never the right man for her,' Sally said
firmly, conveniently forgetting that for the past year
she'd been quite certain that her friend would
eventually decide to marry the young doctor. 'In fact,
now that Amber is no longer available, I can think
of one or two other girls who'd be just about perfect
for him.'

'Hold it!' Rose grinned. 'We'll both have to stop
matchmaking, because it's obviously a pure waste of
time! Just look at Amber and Max. *They* didn't need
anyone's help to get together.'

'Oh, I don't know...' her friend murmured,
nodding towards where Mr Glover, the house agent,
was pursing his lips as he frowned suspiciously down
at some of the oak panelling in the hall. 'I know it
might seem a bit far-fetched...but old "Gloomy
Glover" does seem to have acted the part of Cupid
in this marriage, doesn't he?'

Grown-ups really did act *very* peculiarly sometimes, Lucy thought as she skipped back across the
floor towards Aunt Rose and Mrs Fraser. Everyone
was very happy today, of course, but she really didn't
understand why these two ladies should have suddenly collapsed into gales of laughter.

'Mummy says to tell you that they've finished
having their photographs taken,' the little girl said,
tugging at Rose's skirt to gain her attention. 'And I
heard my new daddy say that he was "damned well

not going to make a speech'' she added with a giggle.
'But Mummy laughed and said, "no speech—no
honeymoon!" So, he's decided to say something after
all.'

'What a sensible man,' Rose grinned.

'And a clever new wife!' Sally agreed with a laugh
before gazing down at Lucy. 'I hear that you're a lucky
girl, and that your mummy and daddy are going to
be taking you off with them on their honeymoon?'

Lucy nodded. 'I'm not supposed to tell anyone
where we're going, 'cos it's a great secret! But I'll tell
you, if you like.'

'Yes, I . . . er . . . I'd love to hear all about it,' Sally
murmured, casting a guilty, nervous glance at the expression of strong disapproval on Rose's face.

'Really, Sally!' she muttered in an undertone. 'I
know that you're an incorrigible gossip, but it's quite
disgraceful to try and wheedle secrets out of a child,
for Heaven's sake!'

'Ac-shally . . .' Lucy lisped, pressing her tongue
against a loose tooth, which had been threatening to
fall out all day. 'Ac-shally, we're going off in a
balloon, and then a plane, and then it's a long, long
journey by boat—all the way up the Amazon!'

'Really?' Sally gasped.

'Really and truly,' Lucy nodded, gazing up at her
with wide, innocent blue eyes, grinning as the blonde
woman made a swift, hurried excuse before hurrying
off across the room.

'That was *very* naughty!' Rose told the little girl
sternly, struggling to keep her face straight as she ob-
served Sally grabbing a friend's arm, clearly intent on

spreading the news. 'I know exactly where you're going, and I'm sure your mother would be very cross to hear you telling such a thumping lie!'

'But I had my fingers crossed behind my back,' Lucy protested with an engaging smile. 'And I know Mummy won't mind, 'cos I've heard her say that Mrs Fraser likes nothing better than listening to other people's stories!'

'You're so sharp you'll cut yourself one of these days!' Rose told her with a grim bark of laughter. 'In fact, I can see that your new daddy is going to have his work cut out, keeping an eye on you! However, I think it's about time we joined your parents. Although I'm not quite sure where they've got to,' she added with a slight frown, leading Lucy through the crowd and trying not to bump into the black-uniformed waiters, busy keeping the guests' glasses filled to the brim with vintage champagne.

'Well, Mrs Warner...?' Max murmured, having swiftly clasped his wife's hand and whisked her away from the crowd into a small book-lined study off the main hall. 'So, how does it feel to be a married woman once again?'

'Since I was never *really* married before, I'm afraid that I can't speak with any authority on the subject!' Amber told him with a loving smile, amazed that such a hard, tough businessman should have looked so pale and nervous during the few days leading up to their wedding. 'However, *Mr* Warner...' she added, stars in her eyes as she gazed mistily up at her handsome husband, 'I can definitely tell you that, so far, I'm feeling *ecstatically* happy!'

'Oh, my darling!' he groaned, his arms closing tightly about her slim figure. 'I know it was stupid of me to even think about it. But I was terrified that you might change your mind and decide not to marry me after all. In fact, I don't think I had a wink of sleep last night!' he added with a bark of wry laughter, raising his hands to gently cup her face, his long, tanned fingers trembling with emotion.

'When I saw you coming up the aisle towards me this morning, I...well, it was all I could do not to shout out loud for joy! I still can't believe my luck at having found you once again. To know that all the secret heartache and deep unhappiness from which we both suffered is now behind us for ever.'

'For ever and ever,' she whispered, feeling as though she was floating on a cloud of pure bliss and over-whelming happiness as he lowered his dark head, firmly possessing her lips in a long, passionate kiss of total commitment before Lucy's high-pitched, excited voice cut sharply through the mists of their mutual desire.

'Everyone's looking for you—but *I* guessed where you'd be!' the little girl said as her new daddy grinned down at her, his arms still clasped about his new wife's slender waist. '*Do hurry up!*' she added impatiently. 'Aunt Rose says that it's time for you to cut the cake, and for the speeches to begin.'

Max groaned. 'Do I really *have* to make a speech?' he begged in a last-ditch attempt to wriggle out of such an onerous duty. 'I don't mind talking to any number of businessmen, but I'm sure to look a fool...'

'You only have to say a few brief words,' Amber told him firmly.

'Don't worry, Daddy,' Lucy said quickly. '*I* don't think that you look a fool. I told Aunt Rose that I thought you looked really beautiful!'

'Well, after *that* vote of confidence, it doesn't seem as if I have any choice in the matter,' he grinned down at his daughter, ignoring his new wife's gurgle of laughter.

'Although, flattered as I am, Lucy,' he continued as he led his new family back to join their guests, 'I must tell you, that if you want to see *real* beauty— together with a loving, tender heart—then you only have to look at your mother!'

MILLS & BOON

*Bestselling romances brought
back to you by popular demand*

Two complete novels in one volume
by bestselling author

Robyn Donald

Storm over Paradise
The Stone Princess

Available: November 1995   Price: £3.99

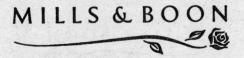

MILLS & BOON

Next Month's Romances

Each month you can choose from a wide variety of romance with Mills & Boon. Below are the new titles to look out for next month.

DARK FEVER	Charlotte Lamb
NEVER A STRANGER	Patricia Wilson
HOSTAGE OF PASSION	Diana Hamilton
A DEVIOUS DESIRE	Jacqueline Baird
STEAMY DECEMBER	Ann Charlton
EDGE OF DECEPTION	Daphne Clair
THE PRICE OF DECEIT	Cathy Williams
THREE TIMES A BRIDE	Catherine Spencer
THE UNLIKELY SANTA	Leigh Michaels
SILVER BELLS	Val Daniels
MISTRESS FOR HIRE	Angela Devine
THE SANTA SLEUTH	Heather Allison
AN IRRESISTIBLE FLIRTATION	Victoria Gordon
NEVER GO BACK	Anne Weale
THE MERMAID WIFE	Rebecca Winters
SOCIETY PAGE	Ruth Jean Dale